Enthusiastic reviews for Lior Samson's novels —

Distant Sons

" [A] book that will stay with me, probably for the rest of my life, and that I know I'll read again. ... It enlarged my experience of being human."   —M. Thornberg, author

The Rosen Singularity

" The plotting is ingenious and the characters come through strongly."   —Rebecca Goldstein, MacArthur Fellow, author

The Millicent Factor

" A solid page turner. The author keeps the pace just right with action and chases ... and backroom dealings."   —RJ Beam, author

The Intaglio Imprint

" Super-realism and compelling rationale, ... an intricate and incisive creation."   —George Church, geneticist

The Drucker Proxy

" An edge-of-the-seat, emotionally gripping, intimate, arousing, techno-legal tour-de-force."   —Phillip M. Samson, attorney

Bashert (The Homeland Connection)

" Samson writes with a crisp elegance, like John Le Carré, and weaves his plot magically."   —James A. Anderson, author

The Dome (The Homeland Connection)

" An excellent read, and very highly recommended."
—Midwest Book Review

Web Games (The Homeland Connection)

" This extraordinary author has the ability to anticipate events. ...
You will not put it down."   —Alan Caruba, critic, BookViews

Chipset (The Homeland Connection)

"[A] multi-dimensional thriller ... populated by flesh-and-blood characters."
- Avraham Azrieli, author

Gasline (The Homeland Connection)

"[A] great novel . . . high concept, flesh-and-blood protagonist, and realistic action. ... [It] will raise your blood pressure and make you think."
—Columbia Review of Books and Film

Flight Track (The Homeland Connection)

"Stunning, compelling, thought-provoking. To the book's broad scope and expert pacing, add three-dimensional, engaging characters."
—M. Thornburg, author

Exit Plans (The Homeland Connection)

"The author handles this tapestry of tensions with his usual assurance and dexterity, which means that I was on the edge of my seat from page one on."
—M. Thornburg, author

The Four-Color Puzzle

"[A]n authentic thinking person's ideal mystery; an eloquent feast of words and an excellent story."
—Jeanie B. Clemmons, author

ALWAYS
ME

ALWAYS ME

a novel by Lior Samson

GESHER PRESS

Gesher Press
Rowley, Massachusetts

Gesher Press and the bridge logo are trademarks of Gesher Press.

5 4 3 2 1

ISBN 978-1-7326091-8-1

Cover and book design: Larry Constantine
Cover photo: "Tribute in Light," Denise Gould, USAF
Set in Alegreya

To my mother, who first taught me what it meant to be a feminist and set me on a lifelong path of discovery of self and other

The only victory lies in surrender to oneself. – Sheldon Kopp

Prologue

With a thud like a gloved hand slapping the dead middle of a conga drum, a confused songbird flew into the windshield of the Greyhound bus parked in the rest area. The bird tumbled to the ground, stunned, before righting itself and flying off. Shanna, startled by the sound of the impact, looked up. Through the glass, at the point of impact, a searing orange stab of late sunlight lit the windshield. In an instant she could see it: a wall of smoke-roiled flame roaring down the aisle of the bus, erasing the few passengers aboard.

Another flashback. Was that the word? Shanna shook her head to clear the image and bring her back from the edge. Did it qualify as a flashback if it was from somebody else's life? Or was it a waking nightmare from another world? The right word was always important to her, precision counted, now more than ever.

As most of the bus passengers stretched and chatted and snacked outside, prolonging their abbreviated pause at the rest stop, Shanna Grace Newsom stayed on the bus, immersed in a practiced past, remembering her new life. Her old life was stored away, as if in some roll-front self-storage unit, a place in the mind that could, in principle, be reopened at any time but never would be. Except for those moments, like the stab of sunlight, that made her think of things stowed away.

Now she was forcing herself to remember graduation day, marching with pride in her deep-violet academic robe with a newly acquired gold hood draped down the back, walking slowly between the rows of folding chairs on the still-brown lawn, past the approving faces of friends and faculty. Why had it been held outdoors then? Because the traditional venue, stately Galbraith Hall, along with half the campus, had already been sold off, she reminded herself, in a last-ditch attempt to stave off the inevitable closing of Kennilwirth University. Not the merger of Kennilwirth College with Mount Cherton, not the bailout by NovaDidaxic, could save the school. So much, she thought, for the efficiencies of for-profit higher education. NovaDidaxic, LLC, had ultimately plundered the campus for anything with a price tag and discarded the rest. History, traditions, archives, everything: it was all gone.

Shanna thought about the man she had chosen as her doctoral advisor, the scholarly and closeted Professor Collingwood, whose heart was said to always have been in the right place and which gave out only weeks after the closing of the school. It seemed a fitting exit line, a cardiac declaration of his true feelings about the whole shambolic dismemberment of his beloved school. His partner of all those years, who owned Robin's Flowers in town, loaded the delivery van with bouquets, arranged them in a giant heart-shape in the hospital parking lot, and drove away, never to return again to small-town New England. Or so the stories in the Boston papers had said.

Shanna also reminded herself of her gap years, her time in the shadows, working at the library, waitressing, delivering newspapers, keeping her head down as she continued to write as an independent scholar submitting for publication, listing Kennilwirth University as her affiliation as though she were there. While she conducted her research online and on breaks at the library and completed her manuscripts at Starbucks, she learned a secret, the backstory of academic publishing in the modern world of arts and letters. Despite the gauntlet of editors and guidelines and the panels of peer reviewers, sooner or later, anything can get published—anything. All it takes is persistence, and persistence was, by that time, Shanna's winning suit. As long as she disregarded the reputation of a journal or the citation rate of its papers, eventually she could get an acceptance letter from somewhere.

Folded into the closely spaced bus seat, she stretched her long legs as best she could and turned from memories to anticipation. On the backs of a modest string of articles in third-tier publications, she was about to join the faculty of a small fourth-tier university and settle into the life she had been slowly assembling.

The remainder of the trip to her new home she spent staring out the bus window, as much at her own reflection as at the undifferentiated and slowly darkening countryside streaming by off the Interstate. She was remembering who she was and where she had come from. She was Shanna Grace Newsom, she reminded herself again, a thirty-something professional woman, handsome by most accounts, born and raised in Cranefield, Connecticut, educated at

Mount Cherton College and Kennilwirth University, with a doctorate in American history, an almost worthless degree were it not for the fact that she was about to become an assistant professor of history at Holcomb University, another self-styled institution of higher learning. There she could sink into the woodwork and live out her quiet days immersed in the last remaining joy of her life: the tables and files and arrays of numbers that spoke an arcane language and whispered to her of their secret meanings.

Part 1 – Shanna:

Chapter 1

The Quad on Old Campus was a white fairyland, carpeted by a snow of fallen blossoms, the residue of a cold rain squall stripping the magnolia trees over the weekend. Shanna Newsom was oblivious, not only from her years at the university, but from her hurried anxiety. As she race-walked across campus from her lecture on economic history to her appointment with the Dean, her multi-hued circle scarf bobbed and bounced. Her anxiety, a lingering fog that blurred the bright world around her, was without specific cause other than her ever-alert approach to everyday life.

Holcomb University, renowned for its rolling, manicured campus, had been repainted by spring, a disorderly seasonal progression that had this year lurched in with sudden storms and cold snaps and days of searing sun to create a beautiful chaos of buds and blooms out of sequence and out of place. Yet, even on days that were not so rushed, the blossoming beauty went unnoted by her.

For Shanna, beauty was more likely to be noticed in its absence, as when she surveyed herself in the mirror each morning. Did her hair need a touchup? Was it done right? Did it befit her, with her forgettable face that her father, in an awkward attempt at reassurance, had once called "not unattractive."

Growing up, she had been average: neither the shortest in her class nor the tallest, not particularly pretty but not homely, not busty and not small-breasted, neither shy nor outgoing, not loud and not quiet, neither a jock nor an intellectual. She was average in everything, everything save one: numbers. While still a preschooler, she had mastered multiplication, devised her own idiosyncratic technique for long division, and had never stopped on her exponential upward trajectory. Mathematics gave her a life of being exceptional, special—at least then.

And now, she worked at being average again, using what she had learned in order to fade into the middle of the curve, to be good enough but not too good. It was a tactic familiar to many women long drilled in how to get along, how not to threaten, how to stay useful but unnoticed. It had become for Shanna a survival skill, especially here, now, on this campus. Stay average, she kept telling herself, but even ordinary people sometimes forget their lessons learned.

As she passed the athletic fields where the women's soccer coach had the team running passing drills, she resisted the impulse to break into a full run. If it were still a choice, she would be out on the field with them, to once again be a mediocre midfielder, but that choice had been preempted in another life. Truly, she thought, those years had been another life.

Dean Tingerly had not given a reason for his summons, only that it would be "a good idea to meet, soonest"—his gentlemanly code for a command appearance. She was already steeling herself for another paternalistic pep talk about her turtle-paced progress toward tenure. You've been on the faculty how many years now, he would say, as if he didn't know or hadn't just looked at her personnel file.

Or it could be about the book. More likely that. Based on her doctoral work, the book was crammed with cross-tabulations, illustrated with scanned historical documents, and padded with a dozen appendices. Despite being published by an obscure small press and weighing as much as some newborns, it had sent the academic sand wasps buzzing. She wondered how many of those among the flurry of fresh critics and fans on social media had even read past the introduction—or the title.

She had been warned; now it was in print. Perhaps it had been a mistake to call it *Built on Colored Backs: The Economic Foundations of Higher Education in the American South*, not because the title was provocative or misleading, but because it drew attention to her. Shanna was attention averse. It had not always been this way, but life had taught her lessons, hard lessons about survival and principles. She was beginning to wish she had listened more closely to those lessons this time around.

At Righteous Hall on the far corner of the Old Campus, she took the worn wooden stairs to the second floor two at a time. In the outer office, at the end of the portrait-lined hall whose old boards creaked with every quickened step, she shrugged and twisted her wristwatch as she passed Bellia Macon. Bellia, the administrative assistant who doubled as tech support for the computer-phobic Dean, was a soul sister, a woman working below her potential but not entirely unhappy to be unnoticed. At least she was, in a shrinking economy, still working. Shanna winked back at Bellia as she tapped on the jamb of the already open door to the inner office.

With a warm Southern smile slathered on his butterscotch face, the Dean of the School of History and Human Sciences stood as she entered. "Professor Newsom, welcome. I am so glad you could see me today." Afsa Tingerly's vowels were like local honey, pure Carolinas, totally at odds with the oddly mixed heritage heralded by his name and hinted by his skin tone. His mother, granddaughter of Pakistani immigrants who had built an empire of motels spread across the South, had argued to her Texas ranch-owning husband that, if the children were to bear his surname, she would get to pick their given names. It was she who earned the first doctorate in the family and who had paved the way for Afsa to follow an academic path. "Do please have a seat,"—Afsa gestured to Shanna—"and make yourself most comfortable."

Shanna worked her mouth into a strobed smile as she glanced awkwardly between the two chairs lined up opposite his desk. This was the sort of everyday choice that could send her into tailspins of indecision. "The lady or the tiger?" she thought aloud, as if she were alone in the room. She chose the one on the left, nearer the windows that looked out over the white and pale-green Quad.

"Hardly that old Stockton scenario," he said, showing off his knowledge of literature. "First of all, I wanted to congratulate you in person. It's not that often a member of our little faculty is so honored. The Sager-Beech Award, best book. My, my, very prestigious."

"Best Book in Quantitative History by a Southern Academic, to put it in perspective. I think mine might have been one of two books in contention this year. The other got the Wheeler Prize, no doubt. I do get a laser-etched plastic plaque and an honorarium, if $256 counts as an honorarium rather than a mathematical metaphor, that is."

"But people are beginning to take notice of you, and that reflects well on this school, on the entire university."

Oh, goody, she was thinking. "And second of all?" she said.

"And second what?"

"That's what I was asking. You said, 'First of all.' What else?"

"You do have a way of, shall we say, pushing the point. The citation by the Sager-Beech committee even used words to that effect. 'Pointed analysis' I believe was one phrase. And so, to my point—ha ha—the Chronicle here wants to interview you for their online edition and their 'History Talks' podcast."

Despite her struggle to keep her mobile face under control, Shanna was afraid her flash of panic was apparent. "I don't really do interviews."

"Now, now, don't be shy about it. For years you've been holding forth in front of hundreds of students every week in your classes. You're as smooth as whipping cream on shortcake, and your student ratings show it. You'll be fine."

"I'd prefer not to. Some of us are just not public figures. Why don't you do the interview instead. You have my CV, you know me, and you even gave me feedback on the book manuscript."

"Yes, but the Chronicle people want to interview the author of 'Built on Colored Backs.' It's the author that interests them, even more than the book. The author who gets right to the point and makes such pointed analyses, don't you know. It's you they're after."

"I was afraid of that. And which are you going to recommend? The door on the left or the one on the right?"

"Are we back to that? No, the Chancellor just thinks that, well, you should represent your own views. It's not the place of university or its public relations people to take on those media people about this sort of thing. Although, we do defend academic freedom, mind you, even when our own faculty impugns our past."

"The book is not 'my views.' It's quantitative history, documented, with numbers and data and statistical analyses. As to Holcomb College—the former Jeremiah Holcomb Bible College and predecessor to Holcomb University— the college not only owned slaves but was built with slave labor."

"Now, if we are going to argue facts, Shanna, let's keep the facts straight. The Holcombs did own slaves, and the plantation was built—in part, mind you—with the help of slave labor—which we all acknowledge and regret—but the plantation is not the same as the Bible College nor the same as this university today."

"The entire Holcomb estate, including slaves and indentured servants, was deeded over—"

"Now, please,"—he cut her off— "let's not get into some academic, legalistic debate here." He held up his hand like a school crossing guard. "This is the School of History and Human Sciences, not the Law School down the road. You know full well what I am talking about. And, in any case, I'm only asking you to talk with these people. Folks around here are very, uh, interested in how somebody from the local university might latch onto what some regard as sort of, well, New England ideas and pursuits. You probably saw the editorial about how so-called Harvard-style history is coming to Holcomb."

"No, but I can guess."

"Look, you know how I feel. I recruited you, remember, and for good reason. I do wish you would publish more frequently and in journals with a higher impact factor, but overall, I'm happy with the heifer I have."

"Heifer? The heifer you have?" Her eyes narrowed and her forehead creased.

"Oh, don't start now, Shanna. It's just the way an old farmhand talks. Remember, I told you how I grew up."

She remembered. And she also knew of the unspoken link between them, that both had been diversity hires on a faculty that was overwhelmingly white, male, and Christian. The school had been lucky to find Tingerly, a person-of-color who spoke the right way and whose color was well diluted. In turn, he had been lucky to find a sort-of-Jewish female hire, which enabled him to tick two diversity boxes with one pen-stroke even after she explained that her Hebrew heritage was on her father's side of the family, and even there, not very Jewish.

Tingerly's eyes grew soft and pleading. "Just please do this interview, Shanna, and make us all look good."

"I'll think about it." She stood. "I have another class today, so for now I'll take the middle door and head back to the lecture hall with neither the lady nor the tiger in tow."

Chapter 2

The appeal to visitors

of Holcomb's sprawling, beautifully landscaped campus was soon recognized as a serious shortcoming by those who stayed on. Nothing seemed close to anything else. A meeting with the Dean, even with an hour between classes, was guaranteed to keep an approaching-forty assistant professor in half-marathon shape. Stergeson Hall, home to the School of History and Human Sciences, SHHS, was even farther from the Quad on Old Campus than Shanna's off-campus bungalow.

The façade of Stergeson was a failed attempt to complement the traditional architecture of the rest of the campus at the time, but it had been built as a science center in the eighties, expressing an angular aesthetic that declared an optimism and a soaring future. With its dramatic canyon-slit entrance and multistory columns of tinted glass, it was a cathedral of science, since passed down the academic food-chain when the ever-expanding School of Science and Technology outgrew it and moved to the shiny new Fairlee Center. The legacy lecture halls in Stergeson Hall still had lab benches at the front, still adorned with their no-longer functioning fixtures for gas, water, and compressed air.

Shanna slowed her breathing as she spread her notes over the black surface of one of those benches. She looked up to scan the tiered seating now nearly filled with students. Her class, Quantitative Methods for Historical Analysis, was a required upper division course for history majors but was also popular with other students, not the least because Shanna had a reputation for being an entertaining lecturer and an easy grader. QuantHist, as it was known among students, was basically an applied statistics course that students in less technical fields could take to help fill a math requirement. Owing especially to students in the applied and technical disciplines, her class was starting to resemble a local United Nations, reflecting the diversity that was becoming the life-blood of the more affordable smaller colleges and universities across America.

Aided by a printout with thumbnail photos, Shanna knew most of the students' names by this late in the term. Those she called hers, meaning those majoring in or truly interested in history, were mostly clustered dead center in the first few rows, their earnest faces for now still turned to their phones and tablets or angled inward to their friend groups. The farther back and higher up one scanned the rows of seats, the more indifferent the faces became. She smiled in the direction of one exception in the fifth row, a newcomer to the faculty, one of a growing number of adjunct professors at Holcomb. They were the Uber drivers of twenty-first century academia, part of the gig economy that gave struggling schools a new underclass to exploit.

She didn't actually know him, but they had been introduced at a reception for new faculty at the start of the term and had exchanged business cards. It was mildly flattering to have someone else on the faculty interested enough in her area to sit through her lectures, but it also made her self-conscious to have him there in her class, especially at moments like this, when he seemed to follow her every move and gesture as she readied to start the lecture.

She guessed him to be in his mid-thirties, not much younger than herself, and an evident misfit in a room with only a handful of older, so-called non-traditional students. As enrollment among the young had tapered off in recent years, the university had worked hard to accommodate older students, but it had few trendy or high-value specializations, and its location, nearly thirty miles out of the nearest city, made commuting difficult.

Surveillance-minded Shanna had looked him up in the registrar's database after the start of the term. Randall McMurphy lived in town, if Taggertsville could be called a town. He had a master's in criminal justice and was teaching an introductory course on the subject while taking two courses as faculty perks: hers and one in cultural anthropology from Professor Belknap. He was evidently dabbling without following any formal program of study. If he was looking toward a doctorate, it wasn't apparent. She had written him off as an out-of-state dilettante with time and money to squander, since no one could live off what the university paid adjunct faculty, especially one teaching a single subject. He did ask an occasional question in her class, invariably good but not always exactly about the material under discussion.

Shanna tapped on the touchscreen attached to the lab bench, calling up the projector on the ceiling, partially dimming the lights in the hall, and rolling down the screen in front of the whiteboard that bore a mottled patina of decades of marker stains. Her first slide was a spreadsheet, with too many numbers in type too small to be read.

"As you all can clearly see from the obvious trends in these numbers taken from Baker et al.,"—she paused while a ripple of chuckles tumbled over the room—"economic output in Mississippi rose steadily over the antebellum period covered. The historical question is: what forces and factors best account for this exponential growth in domestic product? The statistical question is: do the numbers in the available data tell us anything of significance? And—what a coincidence?—that is exactly the question asked in your homework for today. So, let's look at various ways one might approach this question, as a matter of statistical analysis, and how one might answer both the historical questions and the statistical ones."

Twenty minutes into her data-dense presentation, she noted an impatient hand sliding up and down in the gloom near the back of the hall. "Yes? You have a question?"

"But this is all just correlation. You are looking at how different factors correlate to productivity, not why productivity rose. Correlation is not causation."

"Thank you, Mr. Bradley, for restating the obvious, something we have come to count on from you." Many in the room laughed. "I'm pleased to know you've learned the single most important but also most elementary lesson of statistics. You are right, correlation is not causation, but how might we tease out from such data some evidence of causation? Anyone?"

Several hands went up, but she pointed to one in the

fifth row. "Mr. McMurphy?"

"It's Rand. I prefer Rand."

"Okay, then, Rand, how can we use the statistical techniques we've been learning this term to approach the question of what is causing or at least contributing to this upward trend?"

"Time series analysis, phase shifted."

"For the benefit of the rest of the class, could you explain what that rather advanced turn of phrase means?"

"Basically, we shift things in time relative to each other, see if productivity later correlates more strongly with, say, something earlier, like, number of slaves added or whatever. *Post hoc, ergo propter hoc*, as the Romans said."

Shanna smiled. "For those of you who are not fluent in Latin, what he said translates as 'after this, therefore because of this.' Basically, he is saying, instead of testing the relationships between numbers matched up at the same time, we offset them in time. And what do you all think of that?" More hands went up, and she knew she had them.

The discussion ballooned into a lively debate, allegedly about the validity of the dataset or about the statistical tests being applied, but also implicitly about politics and culture—and racial biases. She finally cut it off near the end of the hour in order to squeeze in a quick demonstration of how to use some of the statistical functions built into Microsoft Excel. "You have the original dataset on the course website," she said, wrapping it up just as the wall clock approached the top of the hour. "I want you to apply the statistical tests we discussed today to do your own analysis of the data, then write a summary—in about three-hundred words of good English—of what your results mean and how you reached your conclusions. Submitted before midnight Sunday. Got it?"

The required round of groans was punctuated by a shouted question from the back. "What do you mean by 'about', Professor?"

"Approximately." Scattered laughter followed.

"No, I mean, like, exactly how approximate?"

"Exactly approximate or approximately exact, Mr. Bradley? Certainly you can be more precise."

Calls of "Burned!" and "Ouch!" came from his companions. He opened his mouth to speak, but Shanna held up her hand and smiled. "For those of you who are as, er, mathematically minded as your over-precise friend, our Mr. Bradley here, take 'about' to mean plus-or-minus ten-percent. Okay? See you all next Tuesday."

As Shanna was exiting the building, someone trotted down the steps to catch up. It was Rand McMurphy, from class. "I'm headed back toward the Quad, too. Can I ask you a question as we walk?"

"I'm sure you can. And you may, if you can keep up. People say I'm a fast walker, but, as far as I'm concerned, it's everybody else who tends to stroll."

"There, that's just what I was going to ask you about."

"About walking pace?"

"No, about you, about why you are here at Holcomb. You don't exactly fit in."

"Mah, deah suh, ah really an' truly do not know what on urth you are tawkin' about." It was the best overdone drawl she could muster.

"Exactly. You do know what some of the students call

you, right?"

She did. She had earned the sobriquet for the phony accents she would put on when quoting foreign authors. It was a form of play-acting, like so much of her life. She liked to amuse students with her accents and her frequent repetition of her mantra: Numbers are not your nemesis; formulas are your friends. She gave him a raised-eyebrows smile but said nothing, forcing his hand. Would he say it, or would he waffle?

"Fake-'em Newsom, that's what they sometimes call you," he said. "I mean, I'm not saying anything about whether it fits. Just quoting."

She was thinking that it fit more than he might know. "And do you, Mr. McMurphy, know what they used to call Holcomb when it was still Holcomb College?"

"Just call me Rand, please. Yes, I do know. I'm actually a bit of a history buff myself. Not an historian like you, mind you, but I like digging into the past. You know, stuff like the story behind places—and people. Anyway, it was called Hokum High, still is by some. Just quoting."

She slowed slightly as she turned her head his way. Close up, his face was more weathered than she had realized. Maybe he was her age. His neatly trimmed mustache had a few salty streaks, and his wavy hair was starting a northward retreat. She resisted the near automatic impulse to touch her own hair, which was just beginning to show sprays of gray, a fact she celebrated. Gray meant gravitas in an academic world where women worked hard to be taken seriously. "You are uncharacteristically blunt, Mr. McMurphy. Maybe you don't exactly fit in either."

"Exactly. I mean, who comes to study at Holcomb? Who

chooses to teach at Holcomb?"

"Do tell me. Who?"

"People who settle. You know the term 'satisfice'?"

"Of course. I'm an economic historian. Are you saying you are satisficing, settling for just enough?"

"Maybe. Maybe just wondering if the word fits. Maybe just making conversation with a professor who actually has something to say."

Her mind raced. You are trouble, Mr. Rand McMurphy. I should run, not walk, to the nearest bus stop. "I'm just doing what they pay me for," she said, "meagerly as we assistant professors are paid these days."

"Exactly. As I was saying. That is the very definition of satisficing." His smile broadened noticeably as he waited for a response.

She looked straight ahead as she picked up the pace again. "Well enough, Rand, at least good enough for two so easily satisfied as we. As for me, I have forms to turn in and papers to grade." She tried to walk just fast enough that it would have been awkward for him to keep up. It worked. He dropped back.

"I'll see you Tuesday," he called out, as he stood in the path, arms crossed, following her retreat, waiting to see whether she looked back.

She did. And he waved.

෨

Professor Belknap was entering Righteous Hall when Shanna arrived. Always the old-school gentleman, he held the door for her. "Done for the day?" he asked. Gareth Belknap, an anthropologist specializing in medical anthropology, had been among the first on the faculty to befriend her back when she first arrived at Holcomb. Lanky and balding, he was nearing retirement and often talked about using his savings to retire in style and begin work on his much deferred first novel.

"Done?" she said. "Hardly. I have these new Q-203 or 203-Q forms to file for the summer session, and I can't make sense of the online instructions. I thought I'd ask Edna." Among the faculty and administration of Holcomb, "Ask Edna" was the universal answer to every conundrum. Edna Pettingale was herself an institution, a spry small woman of indeterminate age, she sometimes talked as if she had worked at Holcomb from the time when it was still a Bible college.

"I don't do any of those administrative things anymore," Gareth said, as he stopped to catch his breath at the top of the broad stairs leading into the administration building. "I wait until the office stops screaming at me, then apologize and throw myself on their mercy, only to learn that they filed the dang thing already on my behalf. Works every time."

"That's because it's you, and you use your mental agility to play the sympathy card with your barely passable imitation of approaching senility. And I emphasize the word imitation, lest you think you fool me. Plus the administration knows perfectly well that you'll be moving on just about any day now. Me, they have their hooks into for decades more."

"Unless you move to greener pastures first."

"Look around, Gareth. Look at these pastures. How much greener can it get?"

"Oh, a lot greener," he said, patting his hip pocket.

"And you planning to retire? Not a lot of green in the

benefits we get here."

"Oh, I have my investments. Just biding my time, taking the long view, watching the markets. I expect to do all right. In the meantime, I'm still doing research, still flying." Belknap was a small-plane pilot who used grant money from his field research on island communities to help sustain his hobby.

"Still thinking of Italy?" Shanna asked.

"All the time. My mother was from Italy. I want to spend my days sandwiching writing and reading between magnificent meals and glasses of good wine on some sunlit veranda in Tuscany."

"I hope that works out for you."

"Oh, it will. Count on that. It's all a matter of timing, knowing when to get in and when to get out. You know what I mean?"

More than you know, she was thinking, but she just nodded. "Oh, and there's Edna," she said. "I better catch her while I can."

Chapter 3

The neat little
bungalows on Racine Circle, less than two hundred yards
from Holcomb's main gate, had been built in the aftermath
of World War II for returning soldiers heading to college on
the G.I. Bill. Those had been boom times for Holcomb College, a leg up on its way to becoming Holcomb University.
That post-war boost had been the last wave of demand-
driven progress for Holcomb. Its transformation from Bible
college to university was ultimately driven by the success of
its most distinguished alum, the megachurch televangelist
and multimedia mogul Harlan Fairlee.

Fairlee had lived large, rising quickly to the pantheon of
modern revivalists, with a network of wholly-owned television stations, a publishing arm, and a line of Christian-
themed products for every born-again consumer and
blessed occasion. Advisor to presidents and princes, husband to a string of ever younger and more glamorous wives,
Fairlee built a vast and diversified enterprise on the message
of a green-back gospel: God wants you to succeed, he wants
you to have wealth, all you have to do is believe—and prove
your faith by your generosity to his anointed messenger,

Harlan Fairlee, and the Church of Good Fortune, LLC.

Fairlee's true genius was not so much in his branded evangelism, but that he did what so many of his famous competitors did not: he died before disgrace caught up with him. He also hired good lawyers and accountants, the best that money could buy. With the last of his wives already divorced and disgraced for her infidelity with his assistant pastor, and all six of them bound by well-crafted prenuptial agreements, Fairlee, who had never fathered children, at least by any of his wives, left his entire estate to his beloved alma mater. To the surprise of many and the delight of Holcomb College, his investments had been steadily and surreptitiously diversified into manufacturing, energy, and pharmaceuticals, with only a token of residual holdings left in the many subsidiaries of his religious empire, an empire that started its unsurprising spiral toward insolvency shortly after his passing.

The echoes of his bequest were everywhere at Holcomb. In addition to the Fairlee Center for Science and Technology, East Campus had the Brother Harlan Auditorium along with Stergeson Hall, which bore his mother's maiden name, and Old Campus still housed the tiny and dwindling Holcomb-Fairlee School of Bible Studies, mandated in perpetuity by a provision in Harlan Fairlee's bequest.

From the entrance gate of East Campus, Shanna swung left toward Taggertsville on her vintage green Cannondale. As she cycled into Racine Circle, she pulled over to collect her mail from the rack of boxes beside the road. She could never quite shake the mounting dread each afternoon as she shuffled through the day's small stack of circulars and bills, afraid she might find a letter with some official imprint in the upper left. She knew, of course, her nightmare would probably not arrive that way, but she needed to sleep at night, and this daily ritual was a way to trick her mind into thinking she had made it through another day.

Her blue-trimmed white bungalow, one of the few in the development that had never been expanded beyond its original footprint, had two tiny bedrooms, a central bath-room with a stall shower, and an inline kitchen separated by a breakfast bar from the front half of the house, which served as entryway, living room, and dining room. The house was good enough for someone who had lived alone for nearly two decades, with one single, disastrous brief excep-tion whose name she could not forget but whose contribu-tion to her life she had worked ever since to erase from memory.

The diminutive master bedroom with its old-fashioned flower-print wallpaper had been turned into a home office because it allowed her to spread out more when she was working. The original "kid's" bedroom, with barely room enough for a double bed and a nightstand, sufficed in part because the closet had been augmented by cleverly arrayed shelves and assorted hooks. She didn't need much; she was going nowhere. Her wardrobe was largely utilitarian with a few essential exceptions. Stored in the closet of her "office" were evening dresses for receptions and required social ap-pearances, business suits for conferences, and her academic robe and doctoral hood for graduation and other occasions of high ceremony.

Shanna hung her jacket and scarf on a peg by the door and went immediately to fire up her desktop computer. Vir-tually all of her historical research was now done online. On rare occasions when she needed onsite photos or copies of documents from paper archives that couldn't be ordered by mail, she hired students to become her legs and eyes.

After the slug-slow boot up of her cranky computer, she began by clicking through to her one daily indulgence, a discussion group devoted to her specialty, where fellow geeks with a common love of applied statistics debated obscure issues and tossed Greek-letter insults and mangled mathematical puns with panache. There was a waiting message, tagged to her, from a user identified as DemoToo: "I've figured you out."

Her heart skipped beats, then pounded in her ears. Should she respond? She was one of the regulars on the thread. If she didn't respond, it was likely to be noticed. She replied with a pair of question marks.

DemoToo was online and watching; the response was almost instantaneous.

> DemoToo: You once worked for Waxman, Gold, and
> Walsh.

What did he really know? Her blood pressure and heartrate soared again as she fought down outright panic to compose a neutral response.

> TessTorian: What makes you say that?
> DemoToo: Your reference to time-series analysis in the
> modul8 package. That was proprietary. Did you work
> for WGW or just know somebody with a big mouth?
> TessTorian: Big mouth buddy.
> DemoToo: Before or after?

Shanna paused to think. When it came to Waxman, Gold,

and Walsh, there could be only one meaning to before or after. What would be the best answer? What would be least likely to lead to further questions? Where now was the comfort of numbers, the warm blanket of statistical models that gave simple answers when she really needed them to help make a decision?

> TessTorian: Long after. Never used the package, but this
> guy told me about it.
> DemoToo: Oh. I worked there. Before. Then went back to
> school. Now I'm a social worker with a pack-a-day
> higher math and stats habit. Figure.

Shanna sighed relief. It was nothing. Just some guy on a nostalgia detour. He knew nothing, and she had managed to keep him from wandering down a dangerous path. On impulse, she switched to another thread where she spent an hour debating with a group of physicists about Bayesian quantum theory. To her, part of the true joy of math was that models and formulae were promiscuous and didn't care what they were coupled with or where they were applied. A stats wonk like her could converse with cosmologists as well as sociologists. She signed off when the clock in the corner of the screen told her she should be tired and hungry. She often relied on clocks to remind her she had a body as well as a mind.

After a dinner cobbled from frozen lasagna and the last of some deli slaw, she worked for a couple hours grading homework and tracking down copies of two obscure references for an academic paper she was preparing to write. Once her ten o'clock bedtime ritual was behind her, she lay awake in her snug bedroom, running through her nightly review of the day's personal headlines. In younger days, she would have finished the day by writing in her journal, but written words could escape the page, as once they had. Now, her diary was scrawled only in her mind as a way of underscoring who she was, who she had become.

She began with the online encounter with DemoToo and worked back. Until the crash of 2008 that finally sealed its fate, Manhattan-based Waxman, Gold, and Walsh had been one of the premier players in the evolving field of model-driven investment, trading decisions based on computer models of the behavior of markets. After their tragic loss on September 11, the firm had quickly regrouped and emerged almost magically stronger than ever. Shanna knew what insiders knew, that there was more than magic to the story, but she also knew that some stories were best left untold. Enjoy your nostalgia detour, DemoToo, she thought. I'm not going there.

As she mentally rehashed the meeting with Dean Tingerly, she realized that, against her better judgement, she would probably need to agree to do the Chronicle interview. She was already thinking through how best to control the conversation and keep it from going down dangerous paths. Prime the pump with interesting but safe questions. Yes, that might help.

And what about that new adjunct, call-me-Rand McMurphy, with his hint of a Boston accent and interest in something more than quantitative methods for historians? What did he want? Her first guess was the obvious, but if sex was the story, why was he hitting on her, with so many younger faces on the faculty? Maybe the gap in years was too much for him; maybe he liked older women. Was that what she was becoming, an older woman? A stereotype, a term of easy dismissal? Or a fetish?

She made a mental note to take another look into his record, perhaps do some online digging, but she knew that even there, names and numbers could lie. Hers did. With that thought, she drifted off to sleep, the image of his face hovering above her, slowly coming closer.

☙

She sat bolt upright minutes before the alarm was set to sound, as she did every morning, even on weekends. When her heart had slowed sufficiently, she swung her feet out of bed and directly into her plush bunny slippers in their pre-positioned spot. She tapped the silence button on the alarm, which she never allowed to actually ring, and began her regular ritual. "Good morning, Shanna Newsom," she announced. It was a way of reminding herself of who she was, as was the rest of her wake-up routine. She ate her yoghurt with berries and cornflakes as she scrolled through headlines on The Guardian website, then caught up on email on her university account. At the top of the inbox was a message with "sorry" for the subject line and nothing in the message content. It was from r.mcmurphy@holcombu.edu.

What was he trying to do? Was this some kind of ploy to pique her interest? She knew better than to reply, but she was beginning to become aware of how many times lately she was ending up doing exactly what she knew better not to do. She tapped "reply" and typed "no worries" before deleting both her reply and the original. She closed the browser window and headed for the bathroom.

☙

He was there again when she left Stergeson Hall after her

last lecture of the day. "Did you get my message?" he said, as he paced her on her way across campus.

"There was no message, so I guess I didn't get it."

"No, you know, the apology."

"Is that what it was? I was wondering. Look, I have to get back to Old Campus to retrieve my bicycle from the faculty garage and head home for a pressing date."

"Why don't you ride your bike over and park it here?"

"Are you now also a part-time reporter for Country Cyclist Magazine or something?"

"No. I just mean, you seem so logical, but you leave your bike all the way across campus and ..."

"I am so logical. Bikes have a way of disappearing from all over campus all the time, except from the faculty garage over at Old Campus. So, do I still qualify for my Spock ears?"

"Okay, sure. So, you said you have to get back for a date?"

"I think, Mr. McMurphy, this is getting a little personal, so let's nip the conversation in the bud and get back to our roles and responsibilities as members of this academic community. I'll see you in class on Tuesday." She absent-mindedly turned back toward Stergeson and waved over her shoulder. "Have a nice weekend."

"How about coffee?"

"No thanks, I'm a tea drinker."

"That can be arranged."

"I think not," she said, turning around again, taking a step toward him, and lowering her voice. "Look, there are rules, Mr. McMurphy, and we both have to follow them. This sort of thing is discouraged, with good reason these days."

"This sort of thing? I'm on the faculty, so are you."

"Yes, you're an adjunct and I'm an assistant professor. And you are a student in my class."

"That seems like slicing the bologna a little thin, wouldn't you say?"

"I don't know about deli meats, Mr. McMurphy, but I do know I like my job. I'm good at it, and I like it. End of story."

"You are good at it, good enough, anyway, but I think there's more to the story."

"Think whatever you like, Mr. McMurphy, but this particular story has reached its dénouement. Period. That's all she wrote. Full stop."

She trotted up the steps of the main entrance without looking back. At the top, she realized she had no reason to go back inside Stergeson, but she would look foolish if she reversed course again. With a noisy sigh, she entered the building, strode straight down the long central corridor and out the back without stopping, then cut through the woods. I can pick up my bike in the morning, she thought. If I'm still around in the morning.

Chapter 4

The mail once again carried nothing of particular interest, which suited Shanna just fine. She cut short her daily online indulgence to give herself time to shower, redo her makeup, and dress for her Friday-night date. The Lewises had been among the first to welcome her to the extended social network with the university at its nexus, and they had been inviting her over for dinner nearly every Friday night since.

Shanna was about as Jewish as Afsa was Pakistani, but when she was hired, word that Holcomb had acquired another professor of "the Hebrew persuasion" had spread swiftly around the tight-knit community intertwined with the school. Mark and Adrienne Lewis, who owned Taggertsville's largest grocery store, had long ago figured out that Shanna's Jewish roots were shallow, but they enjoyed her company. She was their excuse to reignite a Friday-night family tradition that had languished after the last of their children finished school and moved on. Friday nights together also gave Adrienne fresh opportunities to play *shadchan* and try out her matchmaking skills. Adrienne was one of those women who knew everybody and was known by everyone, who could always be relied upon to know who was pursuing, who retreating, who was on the rise and who on the way down. Among her friends, she was a walking, talking small-town newspaper in a pixie cut.

Despite the age difference, Adrienne had become the closest Shanna had to a woman friend. Within limits, they confided in each other, but the confidences were of the casual sort. Shanna knew that Adrienne had settled for Mark and small-town life, and Adrienne knew that Shanna had settled for life alone, but neither knew the other's reasons.

Shanna tipped her cab driver and strolled up from the circular drive in front of the Lewises' Greek-revival house. Flanked by the faux-marble two-story columns with waist-high planters to either side of the entry, Adrienne stood waiting in the open double doorway. "Welcome, welcome. *Shabbat shalom*," she said. They hugged and exchanged cheek kisses. "Guess what. My cousin David is down from Chapel Hill on business, so it's a special occasion. He's some kind of a scientist at Research Triangle Park, but I've no idea what he does. It's something like all that numbers stuff you do." She passed her palm above her head. "Above my paygrade."

Shanna was well aware that Adrienne, who worked the what-do-I-know role whenever convenient, was actually the smarter of the two Lewises. Mark looked to her to manage finances for both the home and the business, and she had been the driving force behind getting the two younger Lewises into top schools and on to good marriages. It was only after daughter Maxine had moved to the UK with her engineer husband and son Robert had settled in Los Angeles with his filmmaker wife that Adrienne had realized the extent of the side effects of her success. With visits with her grown children spaced ever further apart, she had turned her energies to local causes and charities, including fixing up Shanna. Shanna had tried to make clear that she wasn't looking for anyone, but that did not seem to deter Adrienne.

"Come, come," she said, taking Shanna's hand. "Come meet my cousin David Jacobi. We haven't seen each other since, well, since Maxine's bat mitzvah. What a *mishugas* that was. Crazy. She did not want to do it, absolutely not, and I thought we were going to have open rebellion, full meltdown, right up there on the *bimah*, in front of the entire synagogue. But she came through."

A deep voice added, "She came through because you threatened to ground her for the rest of the year and then bribed her with the promise of a horse." It was Mark, coming in from the dining room, drink in hand. "Shabbat shalom, Shanna. You look lovely tonight. Did you know David was going to be here?"

"No, Adrienne never warns me. I think she's afraid that if she does, I'll be a no-show. But here I am."

"Here you are, and so is Adrienne's cousin, who is out on the back porch with his pre-dinner bourbon, enjoying the sunset. Come join us. Can I get you something?"

"White wine, if you have it."

"As if we would ever be without it. Adrienne will have nothing to do with mixed drinks or red wine."

Cousin David turned out to be a tall, soft-spoken recent divorcee given to nods and gnomic answers. "So, you're a chemist?" Shanna asked him as he sipped his bourbon and stared out over the back garden now coming alive with early flowers.

Nod.

"What sort of chemistry do you do?"

"Bio. When I do."

"David heads a laboratory doing really hush-hush research," Adrienne elaborated for him. "He keeps us up-to-date on how things are going, but I don't pretend to know what it all means."

"Mmm." Double nod from David.

In the kitchen after dinner, Adrienne leaned toward Shanna and asked, "So, what do you think?"

"Thoughts. Yes, that's mostly what I think these days."

"No, silly, I meant about David. What do you think of David?"

"I think he's nice enough, but it isn't all that hard to see why his wife might have left him."

"What do you mean."

"Mmm." She smiled and nodded.

"Look, some men can be slow to loosen up. Give him time. He's in town for most of the week. Maybe, like tomorrow, or even Sunday, you could, well, show him around."

"Around Taggertsville? What would we do for the second five minutes?" She nodded. "Mmm?"

Adrienne playfully snapped the dishtowel toward her. "Now you stop that. At least admit he's kinda cute."

"Admitted. And kinda young."

"Well, you know, that can be a good thing too, especially these days. That worn-out old formula of older men with younger women can set the tongues wagging, if you know what I mean."

Shanna put on a serious face and nodded slowly. "Mmm."

The evening ended on a painfully awkward note, as

Adrienne maneuvered David into driving Shanna home even over her protests that it would be out of his way. They drove in silence except for Shanna's directions of how to get out onto the highway and where to turn on the back way toward the university. At her house, she was already reaching for the door handle as the car rolled to a stop.

"Thanks for the ride," she said. "And I'm sorry for all that. Adrienne means well."

"Sure," he said, staring down at the gear shift. "I ... I'm not that good. With people I mean. Numbers I can do."

"Me too."

"Really?"

"Yeah, I'm a stats wonk."

"Really? Adrienne said you were an historian."

"I am: quantitative history. I number crunch with dated data."

He laughed. "Dated data. That's good." He fiddled with the knob on the shift lever. "Adrienne thinks I should ask you out."

"And what do you think?"

"I think I'll email you about statistics. It's cool stuff." He looked up, and his face started to come alive. "My lab is under contract to the EPA, trying to extract a signal from noisy data on trace persistent organic contaminants in ground water. You might find that interesting."

"I might at that. Thank you, David." She touched his hand atop the shift. "You're a sweet guy."

The rest of her weekend passed in a haze of anxious self-recrimination and snacking on tortilla chips with supermarket guacamole washed down by generous quantities of box wine. It was not like her to crash like this, not in the spring. In the fall, yes. "And fall, when nature dies, but death does not come quietly," she quoted to herself a poem, a favorite of an old friend. No, fall comes with a crash, a crush, a rush of falling leaves, of falling bodies, of ...

Now there were these people falling into her life, her settled simple life. Shanna had no intention of following up with David, even after Adrienne texted her to say how impressed David had been and that he had even sent her email to thank her for the dinner and introduction, email that Adrienne forwarded to be sure Shanna had his email address.

Even if David had been a charming conversationalist as well as a stats fanatic, it would not have been worth the risk. She had a life at Holcomb: quiet, interesting without being too interesting, and relatively safe. Yes, she missed waking up with someone beside her. Yes, she missed comparing notes over a cup of tea at the end of the day. And yes, most definitely, she missed having a man on top of her or under her. But none of that added up to enough to outweigh what was at stake. She had tried letting someone into her life once, but Guy had been a mistake, a mistake so costly that she would not use his real name, even to herself. He had become just a guy, that guy, so in her mind she called him Guy. Her involvement with Guy was a mistake that had nearly cost her everything, a mistake that she was determined not to repeat.

By late afternoon Sunday, she had made scant progress on writing her new journal article and was reduced to digging out crushed veggie chips from the bottom of the bag and tipping the wine box all the way over in an attempt to drain the last of the generic white. In her current state, she did not trust herself to bike to Shelley's, the gas-and-mini-mart three miles down the road that was her main source of groceries.

"Time to get a grip, girl," she told herself. A run and a shower would do her good, followed by a big mug of Dil-mah's Extra Strong, her go-to tea of choice for lifting her out of such pits of self-pity. She changed into her jogging clothes, pulled on a windbreaker, and headed out the front door. There was a footpath at the upper end of Racine Circle that wended its way directly to the university's athletic fields where Shanna could use her faculty keycard to let herself through the gate and do laps around the track. She was nearly to the end of the uphill stretch when she heard foot-falls approaching from behind. As she picked up her pace and headed out onto the open field ahead, she felt for the keychain tucked in her waistband. It was missing.

Chapter 5

"Hey!. Slow down. Who do you think you are, Joanie Benoit? You dropped this."

Shanna glanced back over her shoulder as she sprinted toward the track. It was McMurphy.

"You're pretty fast, you know," he said, panting, forcing out the words as he caught up.

"And you're pretty persistent. I might have to file one of those Title IX reports after all."

"I'm not stalking you, if that's what you think. I just like trail running, and I do this loop at least a couple times a week, starting and ending at the athletic center. Not many places to run in Taggertsville."

"Hambley Park."

"I suppose. If you don't mind dodging dog shit. Not as pretty and too many people. So, do you do the circle trail, too?"

"No, I was just cutting up from my place to do laps on the track. Running alone through the woods may be fine for you, but ..."

"There's no one around, it's all university land. What's the problem?"

"Deedee Conners, for one."

"Who?"

"A coed whose body was found in these very woods not three years ago. They never caught the guy who raped and strangled her. And there's been others. One woman, they never even found her body, just a torn piece of her dress with blood on it. It's different for women. We have to be looking over our shoulders a lot more than you guys."

"Well, we could run together. It can be nice having a running partner. We don't even have to talk. You can set the pace."

"I don't know. I usually lap the oval. It's boring, but it works. Besides, aren't you just returning?"

"First time around. I try to do at least ten-K, twice around. You're welcome to join me. It's up to you." He veered off toward the tree line at an easy jog.

"I don't know. I ..."

"Suit yourself." He called back, picking up his pace.

"Okay, okay." She sprinted to catch up with him, all the time wondering why she was not running the other way. What was there about him? "You lead. You know the way."

"Holler if I get too far ahead, or honk your horn if I'm too slow for you. Oh, by the way, here are your keys." He reached back and handed her a jangling keychain. "That's an interesting assortment, especially that old fashioned skeleton key."

Shanna felt her face flush. The tip of the heavy key had been filed to a point. "Insurance," she said, "for late-night walks alone."

"You live life on insurance, Professor Newsom, so well protected by your many policies."

And with good reason, she was thinking, starting with you. "Just run, Professor McMurphy, just run."

"Okay, try and keep up."

☙

The trail through the back of the campus reached a clearing at the top of Speen's Hill before swinging around the backside, over a spring-fed stream and across again, then following an old fire road back to the athletic fields behind East Campus. Shanna, used to running around the track oval or on back streets, was slowed by the constant change of terrain and by the attention required to negotiate all the rocks and roots. On the open stretch before reaching the athletic center, she put pedal to the metal and closed the twenty-foot gap to reach the gate just behind Rand. "That was good," she said, catching her breath.

"Yeah, and it made me feel so much safer knowing you had my back."

"Sometimes I don't know what to make of you. I'm not certain whether you're serious or mocking me."

"Yeah, both maybe. But a certain uncertainty is not necessarily bad."

"And now you're an aphorism-armed philosopher as well as a criminologist."

"I'm neither, not a philosopher and definitely not a criminologist."

"But you have a degree, and that's what you're teaching here."

"Those who can, do it, and the rest of us teach. No offense to professors of history, mind you. Besides, it's all about market forces, you know, supply and demand; the market demands and I supply. In this case, criminology is what Holcomb demanded I teach. I tried to wrangle a bigger paycheck as an incentive but had to settle for discount courses. That works. I like learning new stuff. *Bonus vir semper tiro.*"

"Okay. 'A good man is always learning.' And you are always quoting in Latin."

"The Romans said it all, the rest is history. Your field. To me, always a learner, always a beginner, means being willing to start over, to do something new. Like you taking the woodland trail. Or having tea with me."

"Maybe 'always persistent' would be more suited as your motto." She started doing her cooldown stretches.

"Whatever. I'll walk you back to Racine Circle."

"You know where I live?" she said, startled.

"Simple extrapolation. That's the direction you said you were coming from."

"Clever deduction." She switched legs and did another lunge away from him.

"Training. Old habits. Once a cop, always a cop."

Shanna froze. "You're a cop?"

"Was. Now I'm a college professor."

Shanna was telling herself to drop the whole thing and get back to her safety zone, but she kept going, fishing for more information. "Where was that? When?" She sat down on one of the benches and retied her laces as he paced in circles in front of her.

"Long ago and far away."

She was ready to let him off the hook, but he continued. "Boston. It was virtually a family business." He stopped and faced her. "My dad was a beat cop in New York City, and both my older brothers were in law enforcement. The toll on my mother was too much. She left for Boston when I was ten, too Catholic to divorce. I followed the next year, too much of a mama's boy for the rest of the men in the family. After high school, I gritted my teeth and followed in the family footsteps by joining Boston's finest."

"What happened?"

"You want a rundown of my collars, promotions, and disciplinary actions?"

"No, I meant, how did you end up leaving; how did you end up here?"

He looked away. "I killed a kid. Then I got out. Now I'm here. But, like I said, old habits die hard."

"I didn't mean to pry."

"Of course you didn't, but you're curious, and that's a good thing. In a cop or in a quantitative historian." He smiled broadly as he reached down and offered his hand. "Look, I promised to walk you home."

"It wasn't a promise, and it isn't necessary."

"Our days would be dreary if we only did what was necessary."

Without thinking, she accepted his hand and stood, a pulsing rush sounding in her ears. "Okay." She took a long breath. "No. Wait. I really think I'll just head back on my own." She looked down at her hand and gently pulled it free.

As she started back toward the footpath, he called out behind her. "See you in class Tuesday." She kept walking.

੨

At her front door, Shanna sorted through her keys and stared at the cast-metal skeleton key with its sharpened point. She shook her head and laughed. It was only an amulet, a ritual object to ward off evil, nothing more, ultimately useless. She let herself in, then undid the skeleton key from the keyring. She dropped the keyring into the basket on the little table by the door, then headed to the kitchen, where she tossed the skeleton key into the trash bin. "Always learning," she said.

Shedding her sweaty clothes on the way to the shower, she tried to suppress an image of Rand, running ahead of her up Speen's Hill, his corded legs marking a steady rhythm on the switchback trail. The only thing sexier to her than a man's legs was his mind. Rand running on the trail and Rand in repartee were animated images that excited and frightened her, that she alternately conjured and pushed away through a leisurely hot shower with the showerhead turned to vibrate mode. She finished with a brief cold blast just as she climaxed that turned it into a whole-body shockwave and left her shaking.

Wrapped in her plush robe, she made a full pot of black tea, filled her deep-violet mug with its Kennilwirth University logo, and carried it to her desk. The first hour of her research into Randall McMurphy yielded little she didn't already know, but by the time she broke to have something to eat, she had struck pay dirt. She ate her muesli with warm milk staring at the screen, terrified, wondering where she could run and whether she still had the courage to start over.

Chapter 6

Monday mornings, the traditional bane of students and faculty everywhere, had always been easy for Shanna, a reminder that she had a life and that life had a rhythm, one that offered a fresh start every week. Sustaining that rhythm was one of the reasons she always taught in the summer semester and, before becoming faculty, always took summer courses. She didn't want to drift off course, to risk falling back on old habits rather than the new ones she had so carefully cultivated in coming to Holcomb.

The events of the weekend had upset her equilibrium, and she knew, if she was to recover her balance, she would have to push herself back into pattern. She marched herself through her rising routine and on to the morning email check. She exhaled with relief when she found no email from Rand, but there was one from David with a link to a prepublication copy of a paper from his lab and a note saying he often posts on a certain discussion group. Shanna clicked through to the paper, downloaded it, and read the abstract. She replied to David with thanks and a promise to read it later. If this is courtship, she thought, David is true to his geeky awkwardness.

She was about to wrap up for the morning and head over to campus when a message popped up from Dean Tingerly: "Don't forget your meeting with Sam Fuentes from the Chronicle at 3 today." Forget? This was the first she had heard of a meeting scheduled with the Chronicle. She scrolled back through her inbox to see if she had missed something earlier, but there was nothing from the Dean or anyone at the Chronicle. She was being ambushed. Asif, with his always-ready ranch-hand references, would probably say something about making sure you're packing if you're being herded into a box canyon.

Shanna made a quick pass through her CV to make sure it was up-to-date before printing it out. She went to the Chronicle site to check out Fuentes and discovered that Sam was a Samantha, with a background in broadcast journalism. What was her story? What was she doing at the backwater Chronicle? A little further digging turned up a controversy when she had been a reporter for one of the DC cable news channels. Her story on Senator Westford about alleged kickbacks had backfired and resulted in the cable channel facing a lawsuit from one of the big aerospace contractors.

So, Samantha Fuentes was tainted goods, now banished to the hinterlands. Her fall from grace had been completed by a messy divorce from Florida real estate mogul Luis Fuentes. Still, she had kept her married name in her professional identity as Sam Fuentes, which obviously played better than her maiden name of Brown. She seemed to cultivate ambiguity about her background that left people free to make their own ethnic assumptions.

Shanna pulled a copy of her own book from the shelf

above her desk and opened it to the half-title page. What would be a good dedication, one that said I know who you are? Shanna wrote quickly and signed with a flourish.

॰

Among the facilities funded by Harlan Fairlee's posthumous generosity was a well-equipped radio-television studio. Where once it had been used to produce Christian-themed audio-visual material, in recent years it had been adapted as a training center for the media communications program in the School of Arts and Education. Today, it was being made available to the Chronicle.

Shanna arrived at three on the dot, only to find both the student-led tech team and a tall Black woman with a Chronicle ID badge around her neck waiting for Fuentes to show up. The woman came over to Shanna with her hand extended. "You must be Professor Newsom. I'm Aretha Barley. I produce Sam Fuentes's podcasts. She should be here any minute."

"Good. I only have this hour free." It wasn't true, not nearly, but it was a strategic claim.

"Well, we're grateful that you agreed to give us this time. I read your book and think it's very interesting. Very."

"Did you really? That's a lot of prep for a twenty-minute podcast."

"Well, I was interested in the subject. I particularly liked the middle section where you—shall we say—sock it to a number of Southern universities by name and use your analyses to show exactly how much of their current net worth can be attributed to slavery in the past."

"I am impressed. You do your homework. I've had critics tear into me without reading past the second chapter."

"Really? I read the whole thing. I minored in Black History, so it was right up my alley."

"And what about Sam Fuentes's alley?"

"Well, she's got a lot on her plate, with reporting and writing for both the print edition and the website, plus doing the podcasts. I briefed her on the book, of course."

"Thanks for that."

"My pleasure. Trust me, not all the stuff we put together at the Chronicle has as much substance as this. It's nice to feel challenged once in a while."

Sam Fuentes, accompanied by a photographer, whirled in at twenty past the hour. "Well, let's get right into it. What's the scoop Aretha? Where are we taping?"

"The small studio. The student team is making a video for practice. I checked the audio and we're recording a multitrack feed from their board. Not as good as a sound booth, but it will do."

"As long as they understand we own all rights. No copies and no distribution beyond the campus. All right, let's do it. No time for a separate interview; I'll write my online piece from the podcast. Lead the way."

The studio was straight out of vintage community-access cable television: a small dais set with two upholstered chairs, a coffee table, and ersatz potted plants. In her chair, Fuentes kept shifting positions while a student sound technician struggled to mike her. "Screw this," Fuentes said, unclipping the lavalier from her jacket. "Just give me a hand mike. Are you all right with using one, Professor Newsom? Just always keep it pointed at your face and the same distance. Talk normal. We're just having a conversation. Okay?"

She waited while the students scrambled to retrieve

two wireless hand mikes and patch them in. Fuentes sorted through a packet of index cards as she waited. "Are we ready?" She surveyed the room. "We're behind schedule, people. Let's go. I need at least thirty minutes of material to edit down into the podcast." She turned to Aretha. "Did you explain that we need five seconds of room sound at the beginning?"

"I did. These kids are pros. They know the drill. You all set?" Fuentes nodded, readjusted herself in her chair, and nodded again. Aretha stepped back. "Okay, we start recording on my signal, and we do a slow five-count with everyone quiet. Sam has first language. Okay." She nodded toward the control booth, then flashed a stylish five-finger countdown and finished by pointing to Fuentes.

Fuentes looked up from her notecards and directly into camera one. "Hello, this is Sam Fuentes, and you are listing to History Talks, episode number ... oh, shit. What episode are we on, Aretha?"

"One-seventeen. You can just continue from there. We'll edit it in post."

"I'm not one of these students. We do it right, from the top. Roll tape again."

It took two more tries before Fuentes was happy with the results and continued on into her introduction of Shanna and then to the first questions. "So, you've written a book—Built on Colored Backs—that's getting some attention. In fact, it won the prestigious Sager-Beech Award for the best book in your field of history. Could you tell us a little of what the book is about."

"Well, the full title is 'Built on Colored Backs: The Economic Foundations of Higher Education in the American

South,' which pretty much tells it all. It's about the ways in which labor by African-American slaves literally laid the foundation stones and erected the walls and roofed the buildings of the early days of so many of our tertiary educational institutions, which owned slaves and used them as well to raise vegetables and field crops and to cook and serve food and clean the rooms. I'm what's known as a quantitative historian, and I'm interested in economic history. In this work, I am looking at exactly what contribution—in dollars and cents—was made by slaves to southern colleges and universities, including the indirect contribution in gifts and grants—such as land—from slave-owning donors."

"So, Professor Newsom, this is a trendy topic these days, I mean, the notion that our great nation was founded in some sort of 'original sin' of slavery and the slave trade. You were born and raised up in Connecticut, right? What got a Connecticut Yankee so fired up on this topic to write some 750 pages about it? I mean, this is not some ancestral agenda about well-hidden African-American heritage in your genome, is it?"

"No, I haven't done 23andMe, but history is history. The history of any one part of the country—or the world—belongs to all of us, has something to teach us wherever we live or come from."

"And what lesson do you think, all this, this 'ancient history' has to teach us today. We don't own slaves anymore, nor do our colleges and universities. The past is dead and gone. Some would say good riddens, although maybe we have lost something as well, wouldn't you say?"

"I would crib from Santayana and say that if we do not study our history and learn from it, we doom ourselves to repeat many of the same mistakes."

The tension in the studio rose and fell over the course of the interview, with Fuentes repeatedly trying to push Shanna into a corner. Toward the end, Fuentes switched from the historic past to the personal past. "So, you are a graduate of Kennilwirth University, right? Your very impressive résumé says you have a PhD in American History from Kennilwirth."

"That's right."

"And where did you do your undergraduate work?"

Shanna licked her lips. "At Mount Cherton College."

"Where was that?"

"In Mount Cherton, Vermont.

"That's odd, because I could not find either of those institutions listed in any of the directories of accredited colleges and universities. Why would that be?"

Shanna stiffened but kept her voice relaxed. "If you check the Wikipedia, you'll learn that Cherton merged with Kennilwirth to become Kennilwirth University, which was later bought out by a for-profit higher ed company, and which ultimately ceased to operate."

"Ah, yes, that's right—NovaDidaxic, the corporate diploma mill that was investigated by congress a few years ago."

"After my time, I'm afraid. And neither the university nor the department of history were ever involved in a congressional inquiry or any scandal that I know of. NovaDidaxic was the parent company that was supposed to save the university—which they failed to do, by the way—that was accused of fraudulent financial dealings and deceptive representations."

"Ah, I see." She shuffled through her cards. "So, you

studied at this small New England college, which had grand ambitions of becoming a real university, and that failed. And now here you are, at venerable Holcomb University, setting Southerners straight about their tainted ancestry and the sins of their forefathers. For this, I am sure we should be grateful."

Before Shanna could respond, Fuentes continued. "And with that, let me say that I am grateful to all you listeners who could join us for another edition of 'History Talks' with yours truly, Sam Fuentes. Until next time, remember, the past is in the present." She set down her microphone. "Whew. Good job everybody. Another episode in the can. And thank you, professor, for an enlightening and engaging discussion. Good luck with your book." She stood to leave. "Let's get the recording, Aretha, and head back to the office. Lots to do."

Shanna reached behind her before standing up. "Before you go, I thought you might like your own signed copy of my book." She held out the heavy book in two hands.

"Thank you, but you can just give it to Aretha."

"She already has her own copy. This one is for you, with a personal message."

"Oh, really?" She took the book and opened it to the half-title page and read the inscription. Her cheeks reddened. "I don't know what to say, so I'll just say thanks and leave it at that."

As Fuentes headed toward the door, Aretha stepped over beside Shanna. "What did you write in the book? Looks like you hit a nerve."

"I just told her how much I learned from the video on YouTube of her congressional testimony. And something about how much we all have to learn from our pasts."

Aretha laughed. "You are good. I'll make sure the edits leave you sounding that way." She winked and left.

҂

Rand McMurphy was waiting outside the studio. "Good interview," he said. "I thought you volleyed her fastballs pretty well, even when they were out of bounds."

"You heard?"

"Yeah, it was on the speakers out here. Got me to wondering how much of your sting they're going to edit out."

"Maybe not that much. The producer is a friend."

"Really? You know Aretha?"

"And you know her?"

"Yeah, I was pulled in on one of her podcasts. She's a smart lady. Another one working below her potential."

Shanna drew back. "You really are persistent, aren't you. Keep it up and I absolutely will have to report you."

"Or you'll finally have to sit down over a cup of tea with me."

"I already told you what I thought of that idea, and I haven't done a rethink since."

"You know," he said, "the interview got me to thinking about our first conversation, about why people end up here, at Holcomb, and I was also wondering how it is that you ended up at Kennilwirth. Why did you pick Kennilwirth, a dying university, and before that, why a failing college?"

Shanna stared at him and slowly shook her head. Why did I pick them? she thought. Maybe that's exactly why. "I don't know. Sometimes an opportunity opens up and we just walk in. It seemed like the right thing to do at the time. Maybe it was a mistake, maybe not. Here I am. And here you are. Still. Persistent." She stepped back from him and gave him a look that would have been difficult to decipher. She was thinking about her personal paradox, the way her pursuit of structure and predictability were the occupying force that kept in check her indigenous drive to move in the moment. "Okay," she said. It was impulsive, but that part of her that acted in the instant had more than once saved her. Literally.

"Okay what?"

"You can buy me a cup of tea, and I'll buy you a coffee. Or whatever."

Chapter 7

The student center in the new wing off the old library had recently been upgraded by replacing the conventional single-vendor food service with a ring of name-brand concessions surrounding a food court. The upgrade meant more choices but also higher prices—and, of course, more revenue for the university. Rand led the way through the obstacle course of skewed chairs and milling students to a cluster of tables near the Starbucks bay.

Shanna looked around. "Why here? The faculty lounge is quieter."

"Exactly. Easier here to have a private conversation. What can I get you?"

"Hot tea, black. But I can get it myself."

"I'm sure you can, but it was my invite, so at least let me play busboy."

"But ... oh, why not, okay."

He returned with a grande latte and a tea in tall disposable cups. "There. Now,"—he sat down and took an airy sip— "why have you been stalking me?"

"What?" She blew on the steaming tea. "What makes

you think I was stalking you?"

"Remember, I was a cop, with a cop's habits. I had my EduTraxer profile set to alert me whenever somebody accessed it. The same on several other people-finder sites, so I know when someone starts digging into my background."

"Wow. And you think I'm paranoid."

"I'm not sure about you, but I consider myself prudent, protected but not paranoid."

"But you changed your name. Why was that?"

"There, so you know I changed my name. You've effectively admitted you were stalking me online."

"You keep using that word, stalking. I just wanted to find out more about this guy who was stalking me."

"You know, we can spend the whole afternoon arguing about who is stalking whom and not learn a thing. Why not just talk straight?"

Shanna stared into her tea, waiting for it to cool enough to be drinkable. The last thing she wanted to do was to talk straight. "You first, then. Why did you change your name?"

"Not much of a change: Murphy to McMurphy. Besides, it was originally McMurphy when my grandfather arrived on a boat from Dublin, but people kept telling him it sounded too Irish, so he dropped the first two letters. Big difference, eh?"

"But again, why did you change it back?"

"Because I wanted to make it just a little harder for people to dig into ancient history without making it too hard for me to keep going forward. Growing up, I was known as Sean, my middle name. Sean Murphy, that was me. I left that whole world of Sean Murphy behind." It was his turn to stare into his coffee.

"You don't have to tell me."

"No, I want to, I want to tell you, but that doesn't mean it's easy." He sipped some of the foam from the top of his latte. "I was in New York, on duty, and …"

"I thought you told me you were with the Boston police."

"I was. On my way to making lieutenant, despite some bumps in the road. Then September 11 hit, and New York City was overwhelmed. Plus, I got a distress call from my dad, who was nearing retirement but was suddenly pulling double shifts. So, me and a couple buddies got ourselves reassigned to go help out in Manhattan. It was only the second day, and we drove down in an unmarked car but with our lights flashing the whole way so we wouldn't get pulled over or hassled trying to get into the city. My dad managed the intros, and then, there we were, patrolling the streets, and I was back in uniform after making detective." He blew gently on his coffee and took a hesitant sip.

"There were a lot of us from out of town: fire, police, EMTs, civilian volunteers. Everybody wanted to help, and it was still pretty chaotic, with search teams in the wreckage looking for survivors and firefighters trying to extinguish smoldering remains. It was hard to establish a perimeter with so much debris scattered so widely. Anyway, I'm patrolling this section and turn down an alleyway. There's this big Black kid digging around in rubble, and suddenly he pulls up a handbag covered in this weird gray-white dust that was everywhere, like dirty, gritty snow. He blows it off, looks inside, and lets out a whoop. I yell at him to drop it. He runs, I give chase, and I'm getting really pissed. Here we are, we've been attacked, a lot of people have died, and this kid is robbing the dead.

"I'd been on duty ten or twelve hours straight by then, plus the drive down from Boston. I'm not making excuses, I'm just telling it. I pulled my piece and ordered him to stop. He did. Then he reaches into the bag and suddenly turns around with his arm swinging toward me. Trained reflexes kick in: I fire, one shot, right for the stop zone. I caught him square in the heart. He died as I ran to him, his hand extended, clutching a fistful of hundred-dollar bills. He wasn't trying to kill me; he was trying to bribe me.

"It was a Louis Vuitton handbag. Some woman, before she tried to flee the Towers, had stuffed her purse with cash. People do funny things, you know. What do you grab when your house is burning down? This woman, well, there was close to twenty thousand jammed in there. Not hers, we assume.

"The kid was fourteen, big for his age. One minute he thinks he has struck it rich, and the next, he is struck by a bullet and lying there, dead. Just a kid, some poor Black kid. And me, an exhausted cop from Boston who shouldn't even have been there.

"There's all these procedures for an officer-involved shooting, and, of course, I tried to follow them, but it was such chaos. And it's the NYPD. Another state, another city. I'm not even on the force in New York. A mess. Anyway, my report is late, it gets misfiled, the investigation is mishandled, I'm relieved from duty—standard procedure—and head back to Boston. My mistake. Now New York wants me, and my Captain is furious and … it just gets messier and messier. I end up stuck on the sidelines while the nation is going to war. I'm being threatened with charges. I'm hitting the booze.

"Then I find out my dad was killed the following week by falling debris. That was it. I let them put me through a departmental hearing, didn't say a word in my defense, and I was out. No retirement, no severance, no career. My two brothers wouldn't talk to me. My mother was supportive and let me move back in with her when I was evicted from my own place, but she could only do so much. After my third operating-under-the-influence, I lost my driver's license. I finally realized I could either borrow a piece and suck the barrel or start over and reinvent myself.

"So, here I am, Rand McMurphy, Adjunct Professor in Sociology, Holcomb University School of History and Human Sciences. I live in a walk-up studio apartment in tiny Taggertsville and drive a beat-up Honda Civic, but I keep busy."

The silence hung between them as they both took slow sips of their drinks. "Wow," she said. She took another drink. "How ... how do you manage? Forgive me, but I'm always the economic historian. Even with the rock-bottom rents in our depressed area, how can you get by on what you make?"

"I don't. I, er, inherited some, a nest egg. And I have a hobby that brings in a few bucks now and then."

"A hobby?"

"Yeah, I investigate cold cases. If you solve one, it can sometimes pay pretty well, especially financial fraud or where there's insurance involved."

Shanna's hand froze half-way to her cup of tea.

"Yeah," he said, "in fact, I'm working on a case now,

some big money involved."

She reached for her tea, but her mind was diving into a mental foxhole, and her hand closed on air, knocking the paper cup over and sending scalding-hot tea across the table.

She shot up, in the process bumping the table, knocking over his coffee, popping the lid, and adding a sticky, foamy, overheated mess to the waterfall of tea now flooding over the side. "Oh, my god, I'm so sorry." She looked around for something to wipe up with and was greeted by a gaggle of students laughing and applauding. One young man in a fraternity jacket looked straight at her. "Great finish, prof. I'll remember not to sit in the front row at any of your lectures." Shanna's face reddened.

"Are you all right?" she half whispered to Rand.

"I'm fine. My pants and shirt will wash. Fortunately, your aim is not all that great, and you missed my crotch." He started laughing. "What a scene."

"I am such a klutz." She stood to the side, feeling helpless, as a young woman busing trays for one of the food vendors made a beeline toward them with a wad of paper napkins. Shanna and the woman had wiped up the worst from the top of the table when an older Black man in a blue-and-black coverall of the service staff arrived with a mop and bucket. "I am so very sorry," Shanna said to him.

"Oh, now, don't you fuss over spilt milk," he said. "It'll only take a minute. Floor needed a good wash down anyway." He started an expert dip-and-draw with the mop, quickly keeping the puddle from spreading farther and finishing off with a well-wrung mop to leave the floor clean and already on its way to drying. "There you go. Good as new. I'd look after that blouse though, ma'am. Wouldn't want those stains to set."

"Thank you, thank you. I so appreciate it. I didn't mean to make extra work for you."

"It's nothin' extra, just work. All just part of my job." He gave her a big warm smile. "Happy to help you professors." He gave her a polite nod, then one to Rand, and wheeled away with his mop and bucket.

Rand looked at her and started to chuckle quietly. She took one look at his wet pants and shirt and started to laugh with him. "Not the reaction I was expecting to my little confession," he said. "Remind me to be more circumspect in the future. I wouldn't want to chance your hot-tea aim improving too much."

"I am sorry."

"Stop saying that. You didn't deliberately dump almost a quart of caffeine-laden liquid on me, did you? No, don't answer. I don't think I would want to know that about you." He shrugged. "So, what do we do now?"

"Well, it's almost quitting time, and I better get my clothes soaking in enzyme treatment if I ever want to wear this outfit again." She looked down at her front. "I do look a sight."

"And I don't?"

She suppressed a laugh. "I'd recommend you follow my lead and get out of those sad clothes and get them to the laundromat."

He gave her a look that hovered between a warm smile and something more feral. "Look, you can't walk or bike home looking like that. I'll give you a ride."

"In your beat-up Civic."

"No, I was thinking of my black-and-yellow Mustang Cobra in honor of the occasion, except, dang, it's being serviced. Look, I'm parked in the faculty garage. We can walk the back way around. We'll run into fewer people that way."

She was already walking out with him when she came to her senses. This is dumb, she told herself, dumb and dangerous. Maybe it was already too late. In fact it almost certainly was too late. But what was his game? Why was he waiting, playing cat and mouse with her? Should she probe? Force his hand? Or was it time to leave town, time to buy time, time to start over? Again.

She rode in silence for the short hop to her house. "Thanks for the lift," she said, as she opened the door.

"No sweat. I'll see you tomorrow." He rolled down the window after she stepped out. "Maybe after class you can tell me your story."

"Maybe."

"I promise not to dump coffee all over you."

"We'll see," she said, as she turned toward the house. She was thinking that maybe it would be better to string him along while she put together some plans. At the front door, she turned and smiled at him. He was grinning, that smile somewhere between warm and feral.

Chapter 8

Shanna, whose dreams were nearly always haunted but seldom passed the threshold to nightmare, spent a fitful night slipping in and out of chase scenes, flash fires, and explosions—and faces in the sky. The faces were sometimes Guy, sometimes Rand, but always with that same look of invitation and threat. She sat bolt upright at the sound of the alarm, its insistent pulse growing steadily louder. It was a first for her to have to actually turn off the alarm, and it set the tone for an entire off-kilter day.

Her morning email check-in revealed a message with an MP3 attachment from Aretha Barley at the Chronicle. "Good interview. This is the raw audio. It'll be cleaned up and edited before posting. I'll send you a copy of the final. Have a nice day."

There was also a text on her phone from Rand. "Stains came out. No problem. See you, Rand." How had he gotten her mobile number? It wasn't listed in the faculty directory.

With an overflowing bowl of yoghurt and strawberries sprinkled with corn flakes, she sat down at her computer to begin the long-term project of her personal reconstruction.

If she was the cold case Rand was working on, it would probably become necessary. It would not be easy, not only because of the emotional toll, but because of the limitations of her life at Holcomb. She would have to draw on her student assistants to access records, and it could be hard to establish a pretense for accessing the kind of information she would need. Was there any way to do it online without leaving traces? It was a classic chicken-and-egg problem. She would essentially need a new identity to do the research without leaving fingerprints, which was the whole point: to get a new identity. She, of all people, knew that anonymity and privacy were both illusions in the age of RealID and corporate surveillance and government monitoring. That was why she didn't have a driver's license anymore. All the databases were interconnected and continually scanned by algorithms and neural networks.

Massachusetts, where she last lived after leaving Connecticut, had been one of the last states to sign onto the federally mandated RealID program. Her old-style license eventually expired. Now she couldn't drive. She could still fly using her passport, if necessary, but planes were a trigger for her terrors. A new passport for a new identity was probably beyond reach. Could she ever bring herself to reach into the criminal underworld for faked papers? Perhaps it would come to that, but before she was ready to turn down that dark alley, she needed to do some research on her own.

She shut down her computer. Maybe she should start using the terminals at the university library, but not with her faculty access. She could log on using the credentials of her student researchers. Lazlo would be a good target. He was graduating and already well into the senior slide. He wouldn't be paying close attention, and his account could probably be kept active for a while after he left campus.

As for cold-case detective Rand McMurphy, the important thing would be to string him along without raising suspicions further and without springing his trap, wherever it might be set. In the meantime, she could keep digging, trying to build a picture and understand what he was really about, get to know his strengths and his liabilities, figure out how to play him.

⌘

Shanna spent the morning setting wheels in motion. Taking a clue from Rand, she set up alerts for her EduTraxer profile along with automatic search-engine queries for keywords on postings that might indicate someone was on her trail. She checked out the library and located a carrel at the end of one row that offered some semblance of isolation. She tested out logging in as one of her students. To avoid accidentally attempting a login if they were already on the system, she used her research team-leader group-chat function to see who was online. There was still the chance that a student might try to log in when she was already using their account, but she would keep her sessions short and better the odds by using her stats savvy.

She downloaded the message logs from her research group, used a package to convert the information into an organize table format, and then wrote a program to analyze the data and look for patterns. From the output, she learned when and from where each of her five student research assistants typically used the system. Christina was out because she kept herself logged in permanently. Lazlo, on the other hand, was a midnight-to-four scholar who never logged in

67

again before noon. A late sleeping slacker, he was obviously circling in a holding pattern until he graduated. Shanna wondered what he would do next. He was smart and always came through on his work for her, but his heart was clearly no longer in the academic grind.

She lost track of time in the carrel and had to hurry back across campus for her lecture at Stergeson Hall. McMurphy was not in his usual spot.

As she scanned the room, she realized she had forgotten to go over her lecture notes on ethical values in historical research. It was not like her to be so unprepared, so she decided to punt. She told the class to divide into groups of five and assigned them a provocative, open-ended discussion question about values and bias in historical research. She gave them twenty minutes to reach a consensus, then fifteen minutes to prepare a three-minute presentation for the class.

"Okay, which group would like to go first?" There were nervous looks around and shrugs, but no volunteers. "Really, no one is interested in impressing their peers and their professor? A presentation is worth dropping another lowest quiz score from your grade calculation. For everyone in the group." Hands shot up around the room.

Some of the short presentations were uninspired monologues from a reluctant presenter, but some of the groups got creative, including one that acted out a police interrogation of a social scientist who had been doing research on police violence against black suspects.

"Okay, class, some great presentations there. That's it for today. Presenters, send me the names and student numbers of everyone in your group so I can credit them. And everybody, the mid-term test is next week. And yes, Bradley, that includes everything we've covered to date, including factor analysis. So, hit the books, people."

Shanna sighed with relief that she had made it through the day. The weeks ahead were going to be tough unless she did something to lower her anxiety. She was gathering her things and clearing out for the next instructor when a text came in on her phone. It was from Rand. "Sorry to miss class. Called away, back Thursday. Dinner Friday?"

It would be a major escalation but could work to her advantage. And it probably meant she was okay for now, at least until Friday. She would have to let the Lewises know. Adrienne would be thrilled to hear she had a date. Shanna texted back to Rand: "Sure. Time?"

She was unlocking her bicycle at the faculty garage when the reply came in. "7. I'll pick you up. I booked us a table at Dahlia's." Wow, she thought, zero to sixty in one date. Dahlia's was one of the best-known restaurants in the county, with a two-month waitlist for reservations. How did you do it, Rand? What people do you know?

By the end of the week, Shanna was beginning to reconcile herself to the prospect of starting over from scratch, even though it would be hard at this stage in life and would certainly be on a down staircase. Lifestyle? Interesting work? Who needs those when the threat is existential?

Friday afternoon was packed with anxious anticipation, right down to which shoes and which bra and panties to wear. As to her outfit, there weren't a lot of options that would fit within the error bars for Dahlia's. She settled on a smart-casual compromise, with a flecked silver-gray suit-top over a blouse and skirt in complimentary shades of blue. Rand didn't seem the type to be bothered if she stood taller then he, but she chose black flats so as not to add to any possibility of imposing on the male ego.

When he arrived a couple minutes before seven, he was wearing a grey tweed sport jacket over an open-collar pale-blue dress shirt with dark-blue slacks. "You look nice," he said.

"And you look like we think a lot alike." She gave him a slow up-and-down appraisal, then did a fashion-model pirouette for him.

"Think it'll work?" he said. "I mean, I didn't want to stand out too much."

"Us? No one's going to take notice of two middle-age college professors dressed like twins."

He held the car door for her, then walked around and got in. "You're not middle-age," he said, as he pulled a quick U-turn in the narrow street. "I pegged you as thirty-something."

"Well, coming up on forty. Trust me. I can prove it."

"Okay, you're on. Show me your license."

"Don't have a driver's license."

"Really? Why not?"

"No need. My Cannondale gets me where I need to go, and when it doesn't, there's always Dale's Taxi or the Uber app. Or accommodating fellow faculty members who drive me home when I drench myself in tea and coffee or take me half-way across the county to a nice restaurant." She gave him an exaggerated grin.

"Very old fashioned. I thought everybody drove."

"Not in New York City, they don't. Most—"

"I thought you were from Connecticut. Hartford, right?"

"Right. I ..." She searched for a plausible way out. "I was just giving an instance. Besides, I know how to drive. I just don't have a license."

"And that's really what I was asking. How does anybody get by without a driver's license? Better yet, why does anybody get by?"

"Lots of people do. That's one of the problems that helps power the right-wing voter-suppression agenda, because the poor, the people-of-color, the immigrants are all less likely to have driver's licenses. Require a picture ID to register to vote, and you can claim you're just trying to reduce voter fraud. It's not that you're a racist." She smiled. She was proud of the way she had deflected the discussion away from her and over to politics.

"I know all that, and I'm with you. But I was asking about you."

Persistent bugger, aren't you? she thought. "I just never bothered after moving down here. I suppose I should, but it would be a hassle after so many years since my old one expired."

❧

Shanna managed to keep the talk on politics—and other people—all the way to the restaurant. Dahlia's was a destination dining spot, alone on a rise overlooking the highway, with tastefully backlit signage that could be seen from a distance. It was a busy night. They circled the packed parking lot before spotting a narrow vacant space next to a row of dumpsters. "Prime real estate," Rand joked. "So glad no one tried to steal my reserved space." He stopped. "I'll let you out now, because once I squeeze in there, you'd have to climb over the dumpster to exit the car."

"What about you?"

"Oh, I'm a parkour pro. Dumpster climbing is just a warmup exercise. You should see me leap the gap from roof to roof at the entrance to Stergeson." He zipped the car in, shimmied out through the barely open driver's door, and joined her. "Okay, get ready for some great food."

"You know this place?"

"Never eaten here, but I know Darlene. The owner's another Boston-bred ex-cop."

"But this is Dahlia's."

"Yeah, my friend thought Darlene's sounded too much like a roadhouse or a vintage diner, so it's Dahlia's, even though it's Darlene's. She's got a bit of a thing about names, her name in particular. You'll like her. Another cold-case connoisseur, except she specializes in unsolved murders. She's a fanatic, never lets go. There's one case from Hartford that she's been working on for years. No money in that, but from the look of this place, money is not her problem."

The restaurant was upscale casual, with an eclectic menu that mixed fresh interpretations of Southern comfort food with dramatically spiced Caribbean-inspired seafood and pork dishes. Shanna and Rand were sipping white-wine spritzers and studying their menus, when a Black woman in a tent-sized chef's double-breasted jacket came over to the table. "Murphy! How you doing? Finally decided to try my place, huh?"

"Finally could afford it." He stood and gave her a hug. "Darlene Shirley, this is Shanna Newsom."

Shanna stood and shook hands. "Pretty impressive

place you have here, with a county-wide reputation. You seem to have made a name for yourself."

"Well, thanks. It's been a lot of miles—and not a few pounds—from where I started, but I made it. Still not so sure about the name, but now I'm stuck with it, just like my own."

"You don't like Darlene?"

"Never. Growing up, I wished my mother had named me something that sounded more Black and trending. You know, like Shaniqua or Rihanna, anything but Darlene. She told me I was named for that famous duo, Darlene and Shirley, and I told her it was Laverne and Shirley. She said 'Whatever, dearie.' She had a memory like a mug with a crack in it. Know what I'm saying?" She grinned, tight-mouthed. "And what about you? You at the university with Professor Murphy here?"

"Yeah, I am."

"You one of his students? Is he any good as a teacher?"

Shanna laughed. "No, I'm not a student. I'm an assistant professor."

"On her way to becoming chair of the department of history," Rand interjected. "She has a book out, just won a big award."

"Oh, right, I know about that." Dahlia's grin broadened. "You're that professor what called it like it is on the history of the campuses down here. I heard about you. Wow, it's a pleasure. Look"—she reached out and snatched their menus— "you don't need these. Let me just take care of you. I'll give you such good food that you'll waddle out of here looking like me."

☙

The dishes kept coming for hours, a parade of small plates with big flavors, starting with an appetizer of buckwheat bread sticks and a jalapeño and roasted green-tomato dipping sauce, followed by cups of corn chowder with razor clams and a drizzle of Creole coulis for the soup course. With each course, the sommelier cleared their glasses and introduced them to a new wine pairing, and every once in a while, Darlene would come out and chat for a couple of minutes. The attentive service was drawing the curiosity of other diners, to the point that one young couple on their way out stopped by their table. "Sorry to interrupt," the man said, in a too-loud voice that spoke of the number of drinks he had consumed, "but can I ask what you ordered? I didn't see a tasting option on the menu. How did you get all that?"

Rand grinned up at the couple and said, in a conspiratorial tone, "I slept with the chef-owner."

There was a pause while it sunk in. "Not really," the man said, a skeptical look on his face.

"Yes, really," Rand replied, as he speared another bite of jerked pork on a bed of baby mustard greens and sour-cream dumplings. "Have a nice night," he said, waving the two off with the back of his free hand.

As soon as the couple was out of earshot, Shanna doubled over in quiet laughter. "Can you believe that? 'I slept with the chef-owner.' 'Not really.' And you? 'Yes, really.' Too much. You have a quick imagination."

"Not really. I mean, like, yes, really. But that isn't why Darlene loves me. I saved her skin when the police commissioner decided she should take the fall for his own incompetence. Anyway, we were just kids at the police academy, a lot younger and, in her case, a lot smaller. It was a quickie in the back of a tactical wagon. We were both too embarrassed to even talk about it until she got married and Pedro asked about the rumors he'd heard. Big mistake. Never ask a question that you don't want to hear the answer to. They didn't last long, those two, but Darlene and I have stayed friends."

Their server arrived with another pair of dishes, each with a mound of something topped with a shredded nest of something else. "And what are we in for now?" Shanna asked.

"Honey-lime cooked pigeon-peas-and-rice topped with spicy crisped chicken. You'll love it."

Conversation through the entire dinner was focused by the food and wine, which became excuses for sharing past experiences. Shanna was soon relieved to learn that she was no match for Rand, with his endless string of stories. She kept him going by deflecting his questions with her own. "So what was it like, the food scene, growing up in your family?" she asked.

"Irish. Irish and poor. Says it all."

"Meaning?"

"Boiled. Beef, carrots, potatoes, cabbage, onions, you name it. My mother was a masterful one-pot cook. Whatever there was in the fridge, in it would go. Pepper and salt, lots of each, cook it all until it falls apart, serve it with—or on—thick slices of bread. I thought that was great cuisine. Put a little butter on the bread, and I was in heaven. Don't get me wrong. My mother was a saint, but she was a one-trick pony in the kitchen. I didn't know food could have flavor until I volunteered in New Orleans to help out after Katrina. Everybody else was complaining about the mess-tent food, but I was in hog heaven." He put down his fork.

"What about you? What kind of food growing up?"

"I ..." It was a question she had never thought of. She knew every fact of her life, every date of every event, but not the experience. "It was, you know, food. New England food. Growing up in Boston, you would know what I'm talking about. Hartford, Boston: what's the difference? We never made much of a deal about food."

"So, we're both latecomers to real food."

"Yeah, I guess you could say that." She was thinking of corn chips and salsa, of yoghurt with strawberries and corn flakes. "This, tonight, is amazing. Your friend is a genius. I've never had anything like it. And the wine. Wow, it comes in bottles and every one is different. I mean tastes different. I thought white wine was white wine and red wine was sour grape juice. Know what I mean?" She reached for her glass with a few sips still in the bottom. "And the wine. Did I already say that?" Her head and shoulders did slow ellipses as she weaved slightly.

"You did say that, and I think it's nearly time for us to wrap this up. Let me get our waiter."

The woman in her Italian-style all-black outfit came over even before he could raise a finger. "Yes, are you ready for dessert?" she asked.

"I don't know whether we can manage anything more," he said.

"Well, let me check with Darlene."

A couple minutes later, Darlene came out carrying two frost-coated plates with dark brown golf-ball scoops of something very cold resting in a green swirl. "Ginger-Chocolate Sorbet on a mirror of Basil-Mint Syrup." She set down the plates.

Shanna slid back in her chair. "Oh, I'm not sure I have any room."

"It's very light, trust me. Try a taste. I'm not going to be put off if you don't finish it."

Shanna slid a tiny spoonful of the sorbet with just a dab of the syrup into her mouth. Her face lit up like fireworks. "Ohmygod! That is amazing. Try it, Rand. You've got to try it." She took another small bite and savored it as Darlene looked on, grinning with pleasure.

"You two want us to call a cab or anything?"

"No, we're good. I paced myself," he said. "But I could use a cup of coffee before hitting the road. And a check."

"I'll get Annette to take care of both. Thanks for coming in, Murphy. Don't be a stranger."

Annette arrived with the coffee and the check. "Is that your Civic around back? If you give me the keys, I'll have it brought around front for you. It's in a kind of tight spot."

Rand fished the keys out of his pocket, then glanced at the check as the waiter walked away with them. "Holy shit."

"Uh, we really should split the check."

"Okay. You're the math whiz. I'm sure you can compute the tip and do the division in your head." He handed her the check.

She laughed. Penned on a diagonal across the check was, "It's on me, Murphy. Darlene."

Rand pulled a twenty from his wallet and laid it on the tray. "Can't always tip as a percentage of the tab, can you?"

"No," she said, adding another twenty to the tray.

The ride home seemed much longer than the one to the restaurant. Despite all the wine, Shanna was animated. "Wow, everyone was so nice to us. And Darlene was awesome."

"That's how it is with cops," he said, slowing to let another car enter from a side road. "It's an all-out, lifelong thing. Well, unless you're on the outs, and then it's also an all-out thing. There's no way back in."

"You mean about that thing about that kid? But you really didn't, well, you know … it was like an accident."

"It was more like reckless disregard for rules of engagement and civilian safety. And I really wanted out anyway. I didn't trust my instincts or my judgement anymore. Enough said."

He reached to turn on the radio and switched to a country-rock satellite station. They rode in finger-tapping, head-bobbing silence the rest of the way back to Racine Circle. In front of the house, she pivoted in her seat and said, "Thank you, Rand.

"No, thank you. You picked up half the check."

"You can be a real tease, you know that? But tonight … tonight was amazing. I wasn't expecting anything like that. I wasn't expecting to have such a good time." She undid her seatbelt and leaned across for a quick goodnight kiss, but neither of them would let it stop. "Maybe you should come in," she said, breathless.

"Maybe sometime. Not tonight. I'll see you to the door." That was it. At the door, he hugged her without a word, then walked back to his car.

Shanna let herself in. She stood in the darkened house, not sure what had just happened. What, in her wine-fueled beer-goggle haze had she just done? Why? And what did Rand mean by his rejection? Was it no? Or yes maybe? Should I even care? We have no future, she reminded herself, maybe I have no future.

She stumbled toward the bedroom.

ล

For the second time in a week, Shanna was awakened by the alarm, except this time she opened her eyes to discover she was sprawled on top of the bedcovers and still fully dressed.

Over a mug of Dilmah's Extra Strong, she checked her phone. There was a text from Rand. "We have to talk. Pick you up at 2. Dress for a hike."

Chapter 9

When she pushed
back the sheer curtain and looked out, Rand was sitting in the Honda. He gave her a wave but stayed in the car. Shanna slipped her phone into the back pocket of her jeans, shouldered her LL Bean daypack, and gave her place a hurried once over, shaking her head at the accumulating chaos. She was slipping, falling off the wagon of the routine that kept her safe. Time to get organized again, she thought, but not now. Now I need to figure out this guy before he figures me out. She turned out the lights and left.

Rand pulled out from the curb as soon as she got in. "Where are we going?" she asked.

"Into the woods, the State Forest over in Utley. I hear it's nice this time of year. And not too crowded."

Shanna could feel the fear welling up in her as she thought of a deserted trail in the woods, but she didn't see a way out at this point. "Why?"

"Why not? Fresh air, good exercise, and plenty of time to talk."

"We had plenty of time last night. We talked."

"About food, about wine. I want to talk about you, us."

And I want to run the other way, she thought. "Those are two different things. I'm not sure there really is an 'us' to talk about."

"And you're the one who invited me in last night."

"It wasn't an invitation, it was … well, it was late, and there was a lot of wine, and …"

"Right. Which is why I declined. Today it's early, the sun is high, and I'm sober as a judge. You look a little red in the eye—forgive me—but still, I don't think you're the type to do hair-of-the-dog cocktails the morning after."

"No, but I'm also not really the type to move quite so fast, last night notwithstanding."

"I hear you." He turned on the country-rock channel again. "You like this?"

"It's okay."

"Just okay?"

"Well, I'm more the Bach and Mozart type. I especially like baroque in the background when I'm working. The metronomic rhythm, the precise progressions. It's orderly."

"Predictable. That's you, as I'm getting to know. You like that, helps you feel safe, in control."

"Now you're psychoanalyzing me."

"No, I leave that to Frau Schmidtlein in psychology. I'm in sociology, remember?"

"And you're a cop."

"Ex-cop. And you seem acutely tuned to that bit of history. Is there something you're not telling me?"

She chewed on her lower lip. There was so much she was not telling him. It was unsettling that a part of her wanted to tell him everything. That was new. The rest of her, the older and far bigger part of her, wanted to scream, do a tuck-and-roll out of the moving car, and then never utter another sound.

❧

Theirs was the only car in the small dirt lot at the trailhead. After shouldering their packs, they set out toward Riegen Falls. It was an easy hike, but the undulating trail was narrow and required attention. They ended up walking single-file most of the hour, without much chance for conversation.

Riegen Falls was not more than twenty feet high, but, swelled by spring rains, it was loud. Water gushed over the edge, plunging with a roar into a boulder-strewn whirlpool. Shanna stood at the lip of the unprotected drop-off, staring down into the cold, roiling water, shivering. She stepped back from the edge and jumped at the pressure of Rand's hand on her back, fear doubling the chill. She twisted away in panic and lost her footing. Before she knew what was happening, Rand reached out with his big hands and whipped her back from the precipice. He held her from behind.

"View's better from up here," he said. "There's a trail down to the right, not as fast as diving over the edge, but a lot less painful. If we follow the trail, there's a little sunny spot with a picnic table around the bend."

She started slowly to relax in his arms. "And you know this how?"

"State Forest website. Oh, I picked up subs and cold beer on the way over. We can have a snack. And talk."

❧

The afternoon sun took the chill off as they sat side-by-side at the picnic table, looking out over the swollen stream. She was expecting to have to parry his questions, but Rand was the one in the talking mood.

"I got a nice email this morning from Darlene. She said she liked you. She also said she found you a little skittish. She was a detective, like me, so it's been pounded into her psyche to be suspicious. Which is good." He took a bite of his Italian sub. "We're working on a cold case together, in this online group."

"What is it with this whole cold case thing? What's it about?"

"Just people who get hooked by unsolved mysteries, mostly amateurs seeing if they can't do a better job than the pros. It's a pretty big and diverse community, but there's basically four types. There's the dilettantes, the dabblers for whom it's a hobby, all just an intellectual exercise. Nerds. They might as well be playing online games or arguing over some scene in Star Wars: Rogue One. Then there are the dreamers, out to become famous for solving the unsolvable, maybe get a book contract and sell the rights to Hollywood for seven figures. And finally the ones like me and Darlene, who can't let go, who have a piece of them stuck in the past. Ex-cops, crime scene specialists, some former spies, insurance investigators, all of them trying to repeat or bring back or stretch out something lost, taken away from them. It's almost a physical thing, like a bit of shrapnel or a bullet fragment that the surgeon couldn't get out of your leg because it was too close to an artery, but it keeps irritating, letting you know it's there, an itch you have to scratch to be able to sleep at night." He paused, frowning. "Oh, wait, that's only three types. I forgot the wingnuts, the conspiracy-theory space cadets, who are not really interested in investigation or new evidence, only in convincing others that some guy in New Jersey was mutilated by aliens or that the guy on the grassy knoll was actually an Israeli agent."

"And that's you, right?" she said with a mock-serious face.

"Screw you. Actually, I'm probably the fifth type, the cynical pro, no agenda or emotional issues, in it for nothing but the money."

"Wait a minute, you said there were four types."

"Four, five? What's the difference? It only matters to the quants. And the auditors, and the insurance companies, and the IRS. See, when it becomes a numbers game, it carries a price tag: a reward, a finder's fee, or a percent of the recovered money.

"Darlene, on the other hand, is into unsolved murders. There's hardly ever any payoff other than some personal satisfaction about justice served or innocence proved, maybe. What I do pays. If you're good, and I am, the checks can come with quite a few zeroes. That's what keeps paying the rent and building the retirement account. And allows me to teach at Holcomb without feeling exploited."

"So, you said you're working on a case?"

"Always. I'm a pro. By definition, professionals gotta keep working. It keeps their skills sharp—and keeps paying the bills. In fact, that's what brought me down here, why I'm at Holcomb."

Shanna stiffened.

"Full disclosure: I'm working on a case right now, here, this very moment." He jabbed at the table with his index finger and looked directly at her, his mouth opened as if he were about to speak.

Shanna, turning to stare out over the fast-flowing water, choked and coughed, sending a sun-sparkled spray of beer straight across the table.

"Are you all right?"

Shanna tried to answer, but she couldn't stop coughing. As her panic rose, her stomach rebelled. She turned away and vomited on the ground behind the bench.

∾

The hike back was slow and silent, with Rand behind, close. Shanna could feel his eyes on her. As she picked her way along the trail, her mind raced ahead. Her fear was becoming layered with anger. She hated him for playing her, for playing with her. Was he trying to catch her in a lie, to trick her into a confession? "You're not going to get me, you bastard," she muttered.

"What? I couldn't hear you. Did you mumble something?"

"Uh, I said, do you want me to go faster?"

"No, that's all right. Take your time. Here, let me carry your backpack." He reached for the strap.

She twisted and jerked away. "No!"

"I was just offering."

"I'm all right. It's not heavy, just raingear and a wool sweater. And water."

"I should have known. Insurance policies."

As they neared the parking lot at the trailhead, Shanna fought not to break into a run. But where would she go? Get home, then get out. Now. Before it was too late. Forget about a new identity, just dive into the nearest black hole, vanish.

At the car, she put her daypack in the back seat and climbed in the front. "I'm sorry for ruining the day," she said, her head turned to the window, staring at the forest with its inviting shelter, its places to hide, to get lost.

"You didn't ruin the day. You just need to get home, rest, take the weekend to recover. You must have picked up a stomach bug or something."

"Why are you acting so nice? Why not just …"

He shrugged. "Look, I'll get you home."

I have no home, she was thinking. You are taking away the only home I had. And I brought this on myself by longing for something, by letting myself open up to someone, by letting someone in.

Chapter 10

Rand was knocking at the door just as she finished laying out her things in neat piles on the sofa. He knocked again. Could she slip out the back? With nothing but the clothes on her back? Where would she go on foot?

On the front stoop, Rand leaned and stretched to sneak a peek through the gap at the edge of the sheers in the front window. He knocked again.

Shanna was realizing he wasn't going away. If she didn't answer, what would she do? She would have to let him in, tell him something, buy some time.

"Just a minute," she called out. She scooped up the clothes and essentials spread on the sofa, wrecking the order and erasing the work of the past half hour. "Be right there." She dumped everything in a heap on her bed and closed the door to the room before letting him in.

"Well, hi. I wasn't expecting you. Or anyone."

"I'm returning your daypack. You forgot it in my car yesterday." He handed the pack to her. "Besides, I was worried. I called, texted, emailed. No response. Are you all right? How are you feeling."

"I'm all right. I was busy. Organizing." She followed his eyes to where a black sports bra lay on the floor by the sofa leg. "Uh, yeah, doing some much needed organizing." She crossed the room, scooped up the bra, cracked the bedroom door, and tossed the bra and the daypack through without looking to see where or how they landed.

"You going somewhere?"

"No. Why? What makes you think that?"

"Your stuff laid out on the sofa, as if you were packing for a trip or something."

"Ah, no, just sorting. It's easier out here in the open than trying to do it in that little bedroom. Sorry."

"There you go again. Sorry. Stop being sorry. And look, as long as I'm here, frankly, I think it's time to stop pretending, time to come clean."

It was too late, she had missed her last chance to flee. Now it was over, the work of all these years. Her life. It was over. She slumped down on the sofa, defeated.

Rand paced in front of her. "This is hard for me, because it's become personal, but ..."

"Just say it." She stared at the worn carpet and the trace of an old tea stain. "Get it over with."

"I hate to do this, but it's business, and I told you, I'm a pro."

"So you said. Is this how pros do it, how they finish the job?"

"Oh, the job is far from finished."

The anger was rising again in her. "Then, why don't you finish it? What are you waiting for, dammit?"

"I was hoping to spare you, leave you out of this."

She straightened up. "What? Spare me? You're not making sense. Finish your goddamn job."

"Look, I said this isn't easy, but I need your help."

"My help? I don't understand."

"It's about some people you know, so I didn't want to involve you. And it could get messy."

"People I know? You mean, you're not after …?" She stopped herself from saying more as she finally began to catch on to what was happening. Whatever it was about, it was not what she had thought. "People I know? What are you talking about?"

"A cold case that both Darlene and I have been working on for years: an unsolved murder with a lot of money at stake."

Shanna was staring into space as if in a stupor. "An unsolved murder?"

"Yes, and the murderer could be right here on this campus."

Chapter 11

The lopsided smile on Shanna's face grew like a sunrise hesitating behind the hills. "You want my help? Is that what you said?"

"Yes, but I wasn't sure I could trust you. And then, when I found out more, I started worrying that you might be involved, somehow."

"Are you going to clue me in? Or is this part of some initiation into a secret cold-case society where I have to figure out what you are talking about on my own."

"No, no. I'll tell you what it's all about." He looked toward the kitchen. "You wouldn't happen to have any coffee, would you?"

"Nope, just tea." She slowly regaining her equilibrium and the world was coming back into focus. "But we could walk over to the student center and get you a Starbucks. I promise to sit still with my hands in my lap this time."

"No, I want to be talking where no one else could be listening. That's what I was hoping to do yesterday by getting off a few miles into the woods." His shoulders slumped noticeably. "Oh, what the heck, I'll try some tea."

"I have this great tea from Sri Lanka with some real

body to it. You'll like it."

"If you say so."

"I say so." She headed for the kitchen. "Come, sit out here and fill me in while I make us some tea."

"Okay." He sat facing toward the back window and door, watching her organize the tea. "You know, you are really one tough customer to decode. One minute you're like a rabbit in the headlights, uncertain whether to run or to freeze in hopes of invisibility, the next, you're making tea for me."

"Maybe what you see is what you get. Anyway, you were saying about the cold case."

"Right. So, it starts when Darlene and I reconnected a few years back."

"Oh, I see. I thought you said it was only that one time."

"No, not like that connect. Online, I mean, on some of the cold-case threads, especially ones that vet their members and favor ex-cops and others with experience, medical examiners, whatever. Anyway, there's this decades-old disappearance of a young woman, presumed homicide, which Darlene hears rumors about after she moves down here and starts her restaurant. She's intrigued. It's a kind of local legend."

Shanna filled two tea balls from a canister of loose tea. "Yeah, I think I know the one you're talking about."

"Yeah, probably. Anyway, Abigail van der Houten was the only daughter of a wealthy local land owner and widower, Marcus van der Houten, whose family traces practically back to The Flood. She's in her teens when she falls in love with this much older guy, decades her senior, whom everybody suspects is in it for the money, because she has this

substantial trust fund waiting for her and she stands to inherit everything after old man van der Houten dies. But the
father is furious when she elopes with this guy—a North-
erner, no less—and revokes the trust and cuts her out of his
will without telling anybody.

"A couple years into the marriage, she takes ill with
some mysterious malady, she weakens. The father visits her
on her death bed. He thinks the illness is somehow the husband's fault, and angrily tells him that he will get nothing,
that she's penniless and has been disinherited.

"Miraculously, the woman recovers. Chastened by the
close call, the husband is persuaded to take out life insurance on his wife, even though she is so much younger. It's a
substantial policy for the time."

Shanna came over to the little table with two steaming
mugs of tea. "Let me guess. He offs her for the insurance."

"Just wait." He raised his mug and held it without
drinking. "Oh, do you have any milk or cream?"

"For your tea?"

"If it's okay. If it's possible."

She sucked air between her teeth. "Just thinking, it's a
shame to mess with a tea this good."

"Okay, okay, I'll drink it black."

"I mean, I can get you some two-percent if you really
want it."

"No, never mind. You know, Shanna, you can sometimes be a bit like a one-way, one-lane country road." He
took a sip of his tea. "Hot, hot. Not bad, though. For tea." He
took another sip. "So, as I was saying, the couple were, by all
accounts, happily married. A few years later she disappears,
vanishes one night while he is away at some conference or

something. The house had been broken into, and there's evidence of a struggle. The sheriff launches a manhunt, a massive sweep of the woods and area surrounding the campus, and they find nothing but a torn piece of cloth with blood on it in the woods on the university campus. The pattern matches that of another outfit in her closet, and forensics confirm it's her blood.

"The husband returns from his trip. His wife is gone and he is the prime suspect. Everybody believes he's guilty, but he has what appears to be a bulletproof alibi—he wasn't even in the state at the time of her disappearance—plus he acts the part of the bereaved husband who's lost the love of his life, his pretty young wife.

"He settles back down to a quiet life of teaching and research, and seven years later petitions to have Abigail declared dead and collects on the insurance."

"So then he absconds?"

"No, he stays put. He's still at the university, still teaching, still doing research."

"I can't imagine who you are talking about. What was van der Houten's married name?"

"Belknap. She married Professor Gareth Montrose Belknap."

Shanna was shaking her head in shock. "Well, he can't be the murderer. He's the original old-school gentleman. So who does your Darlene think actually did it?"

"Belknap. She thinks she's found holes in his alibi along with circumstantial evidence linking him to the disappearance."

"And where do you come into this? You're not the murder maven. I thought you said your beat was financial fraud, that sort of thing."

"Yes, well here's where it gets really interesting, because our modest-living professor is surprisingly well off. Do you know he owns his own plane, a four-seater Cessna, customized for extended range? He uses it in his anthropology research—the grants cover fuel, maintenance, and the like—but he owns it outright. How many professors at small third-tier universities own a plane?"

"Fourth-tier and falling. I don't see Holcomb still as Holcomb for many more years."

"But you're here."

"Back to our first conversation about satisficing and why people settle."

"No, back to our Professor Belknap and where I come in. See, Belknap manages his stock portfolio and has a self-directed retirement account. He calls all the shots, every buy and sell, and he has done very well, so well that he has attracted some attention."

"Tax fraud?"

"No, he has been absolutely clean, files on time and pays every penny owed, has survived two audits and a review of his grants and finances by the University's board of overseers. No, he has played absolutely by the book. I only know about him because of this cold-case denizen who writes computer programs that search open-source data looking for patterns in stock-market trades, patterns that are statistical anomalies. It seems our professor has an uncanny ability to know when to buy just before a stock takes off and sell just before it tanks. He never sells short. His trades are never really big ones that would attract the usual scrutiny, and never with any company that it would seem he has any connection with. If we are right, this man is neither impatient nor greedy. He stays below the radar and bides his time, building his assets steadily and substantially by well-timed trades."

"Insider trading, huh?"

"Except there has been no direct connection between him and any of the companies he has traded in. And very few repeats, which you would expect if he had regular inside sources."

"So maybe he's just good."

"Not likely. No, there's something fishy here, and both Darlene and I are convinced it's right under our noses, right here at the University."

"So, wow." The surprise in her voice was mixed with relief. "What do you want from me? You want me to spy on the man or something?"

"Sort of. Darlene and I are already working the databases, the contemporary online records, and we're both good as internet sleuths, but we want you to be our historian. You're used to digging further into the past. We want you to see what you can dig up on campus. I thought I could do that myself, but I'm too new, too much an outsider to academia. You know this world, you've been a part of it all these years. Plus, your forte is economic history. Darlene agrees; we both want you on our team."

Shanna almost dropped her tea. Her world, plummeting into a black hole one minute, was the next being launched into a new orbit, transformed before her eyes. It was time to take her time and get a feel for what was happening, to play along. "Uh, okay," she said, trying to keep from sounding too eager. "Tell me more."

᳄

Where to start was the question. Historical research needs a point of entry: a person, a place, an era, an event. Belknap was as good a starting place as any, and this point of entry was conveniently right next door. Where did he come from? What did he do? Who did he know. Several hours of digging through university archives led nowhere particularly interesting. He was, as Rand had claimed, squeaky clean. The same conclusion followed from county records, which she checked even though Rand had said he and Darlene had those resources covered. The man had never so much as spit on the sidewalk. There had been no accusations of sexual harassment, no speeding tickets, no disciplinary actions. He led the charmed life of an aging boy scout. His publishing record was like hers: solid but undistinguished. He was respected in his field of medical anthropology with a moderate level of citations in his specialty, the culture of faith and healing in island communities. He made regular research forays doing ethnography among communities in the Caribbean islands and, overall, was away from campus almost as much as he was there. University records showed field trips taking students and research assistants by small plane to many islands. It was his plane, as she now knew, but that was not in the record.

She finished the afternoon with only a general impression of Belknap as a satisficer: much like her, only with a much higher net worth. Why do people satisfice? That was the question that had begun the whole thing with Rand. Why? Because they lack ambition? Or, like her, to keep their heads down, to fly below the radar, to avoid scrutiny. Was that the story with Professor Belknap? Did he, too, have something to hide?

She went back to his faculty page to take another look through his CV and publications, and there it was, right under his name, a truly distinguishing fact. His office was not a room number in Stergeson or in Righteous Hall, or even over in the Fairlee Center. No, there it was. Office: Residence, Deacon's House, Old Campus. Hours: Monday-Thursday, 11:00am-12:00pm. He lived in and worked out of one of the oldest buildings on campus, a small house that predated even the bible college.

She had her hook as an historian. She already knew some of the backstory from her research on the role of slaves on the plantation and in the bible college. She had the perfect excuse to dig deeper.

☙

"Ah, there you are, Professor Belknap." She hurried down the hallway to catch him before he got lost in the inner maze of the Stergeson classrooms and labs. "I haven't seen you all week. I've been looking for you."

"Have you, now. Well you would have needed some pretty fancy binoculars to have seen me. I was in Bermuda all week, setting up for another season of fieldwork."

"Well, good for you. I spent the weekend recovering from a stomach bug. So, did you fly down?"

"Yes, I flew over. It's basically east of here. Unless you're a sailor, the only way is by plane. And you wanted something from me?"

"Yes, a favor. I want you to invite me over to your place."

"Well, now, I know that younger cohorts have adopted this more unhesitant approach to these matters, but that is a rather bold proposition."

"Bold, maybe; proposition, no. You know my book, of course, my research on the antebellum history of Southern colleges and universities."

"I do. Rather respectable work, old-guard sensibilities notwithstanding. And?"

"And you actually live in a piece of that history. I was wondering if I might visit, get a firsthand feel for the Deacon's House."

"Most certainly. My office hours are on my faculty page. You're welcome to pick the day." He cocked his head. "You look disappointed."

"I'm sorry. I don't mean to be so rude. Or so transparent. I was hoping to actually spend some time there, exploring, talking with you about the experience of living in a piece of living history."

"It's drafty in winter and spring, stuffy in summer and fall. Creaky all year round. That's what it's like. And the rooms are all too small except for the former summer kitchen, which is now only used for storage."

"I meant—"

"I know what you meant, Shanna. And I'm only regretting I didn't long ago think of inviting you over for an after-school cocktail or even dinner. My cook is excellent. Shall we say Thursday, around four, just after your last class?"

"Well, now, that is gracious of you considering how blunt I was. I hope it wouldn't put you off if I brought along my camera. I want to add to my collection of photos of local historical material."

"I just turned seventy-four. I don't think I qualify as historical material. Not yet."

"I meant …"

"Of course." His grin broadened. "I know what you meant, and certainly by now you know what an old tease I am. I'll see you on Thursday, then."

I'm in, she thought. We're in. She couldn't wait to tell Rand. She couldn't wait to get back to her office and search through her photocopies of maps and architectural diagrams. She was picturing one in particular, an early plan view of the Deacon's House, with the dashed lines showing a tunnel connecting the cellar to another building not shown.

 ➽

Shana dressed as though for an afternoon faculty reception, slung her Nikon over her shoulder, and walked the entire way to Deacon's House on a rise behind Old Campus. The house, built for Deacon Bartholomew Taggert, dated from the time of the American Revolution. It's broad front porch and an addition to the side were Civil War-era embellishments. There was no door knocker, and Shanna couldn't find a buzzer. Then she noticed a pull-cord to the right. She was about to tug it when Gareth Belknap opened the door. "It doesn't work, not since before my time. Please come in. You are looking quite lovely this evening, if an old man can be allowed to say that without risking a report being filed against him."

"You can risk it and rest easy. Thank you again for having me over." She stepped into a parlor furnished entirely in what looked to be genuine antiques. "Are those chairs Hitchcock?"

"Those, yes. The rocker, though, was handmade by one of the Taggert boys, 1830 or so."

"This is like a museum. And you live here."

"Well, I do have to put up with it being open to the public for a week twice a year, but so far I've managed to be away on field research whenever those dates roll around. And, one has to exercise a certain care. My bedroom and office are in the annex that was not built until much later. The interior of the annex has been modernized, and I have more latitude there."

"So, you own this place?"

"Oh, no, dear. I just lease it from the university. Once I retire, I'm out on the street, so to speak. And believe me, the Board is certainly keeping their eyes on the calendar. End of the year."

"And then it's off to Tuscany, right?"

"Warm sun, gentle breezes: absolutely. So, would you like me to show you around before dinner. The place is small, but I would imagine of some interest to an historian."

"Absolutely, I'd love a personal tour, and do tell me what you know of the history."

"It's all in the little booklet the university prints for their tours. I can probably find a copy for you here somewhere."

"Of course, but I'm interested in your history here as well. You've been here, how long? You were married when you moved in, right?"

"Newlyweds. Well, practically. I can see you already did some research."

"I'm an historian; you'll have to forgive me. Your wife ...."

"Abby, yes, she's such a wonderful woman. Was."

"You never remarried?"

"No. I'm a one-woman man. There simply is no other woman for me." He took a long slow breath.

"You miss her."

"Every day without her. But, don't mourn. It's been a rich life, and it isn't over yet. I have no regrets." He gestured. "Here, this way to the library for the start of a quick unofficial tour, then a drink on the back patio, then dinner."

The library was finished in dark woods. Only the wall housing the fireplace was not fitted with built-in floor-to-ceiling bookshelves. Shanna walked to the nearest stack, twisted her head, and started shelf-reading titles. "Magray and Demple, *A Jamaican Herbalist*. Markham, *Medicinal Plants of the Caribbean*. Mukherjee, McLane, and Wilson, *Toxicology of Tropical Plants*. Wow, alphabetical order within Dewey Decimal."

"Yes, that entire shelf is 581. You were a librarian?"

"In another life. Part time. I worked in a library and spent more hours there than I could count. These are your books or the university's?"

"Some of each. I have quite a few on permanent loan as a faculty member, but the majority are mine. Most of that shelf, which is rather closely related to my ethnographic work on health and medicine in the Caribbean, are my own. But I don't imagine medical anthropology is of terribly great interest to you. Through here back to the hall. I'll show you the Deacon's bedroom, then on to the old kitchen before we retreat to the back patio."

"Isn't there a second floor?"

"Yes, the nursery and the children's rooms, but I have no need, so we keep that closed off, except during tour time."

"And I believe there was a cellar?"

"Was. It was filled in long ago. In fact, I believe the

doorway to the stairwell was over on that wall someplace, but I'm not certain. In any case, I've never seen it. Maybe after they evict me, someone from archeology will launch a local dig." He laughed a deep hearty laugh. "There is so much history around these parts, that you could barely turn a spade without uncovering old bones or bullets."

Shanna walked over to the wall he had indicated and tapped on a space between shelves. "They always do that in the old movies," she said. "Looking for the hollow sound of a hidden passage, I guess."

"I wouldn't know, never having been too much drawn to cinema. But we should move along or Tereza will be unhappy having to keep dinner warm for too long."

"That's right, you said you have a cook."

"The university has a cook. As I said, I only lease the place. I think it's a preservation thing. They probably don't trust me not to bring disaster if they let me in the kitchen."

Chapter 12

"What happened?"

Rand asked, as he finished the last of the tea in his cup.

"I got a tour. I took pictures. We had dinner. We talked. I showed him the plan drawings. He said the cellar had been filled in long ago, and he assumed the same was true of the tunnel. He showed me the place where the original access to the cellar had been plastered over. He couldn't remember when, he said, and he was getting visibly uncomfortable. I watched him closely, but I let it go. Afterwards, we had a glass of port sitting on the porch swing—very civilized—and I walked back here."

"So, what's this thing about this tunnel all of a sudden?"

"I think that's where she's buried, where he buried Abigail."

"But the torn cloth with her blood on it was found in the woods."

"But they never found her body in the woods. The piece of cloth was misdirection, throwing everyone off the scent, even the bloodhounds."

"Mmm. I suppose it's plausible. But it's speculation."

"Look,"—she stood up and started pacing —"all we have

to do is open up the tunnel, and it's no longer speculation."

"Is this how you do your quantitative history? Jump to conclusions and rush to judgment?"

"Of course not." She was indignant.

"Then don't do it with this. We need to put together a case and systematically eliminate other hypotheses. Right now we have questions but no answers. How the hell is this professor living in that house? I can see you're getting excited by what feels like detective work, but this is not like those Amazon originals or some Netflix series. This is more like your regular research: methodical, slow, one data point after another until you can draw a line connecting the dots."

"Well," she sighed, "I guess I've been schooled."

"Don't get bent out of shape, and don't take it personally. We're partners, now. Partners don't pull punches. Partners keep each other on their toes."

"Okay, partner, what have you come up with?"

He did a palm-up shrug. "Not a lot. This guy I know—he's not on the team, too much of a needy nerd—is looking for other investors who made similar trades at roughly the same times as our professor. It might pay off, but I'm putting my chips down on your historical research."

He stood and put his tea cup in the sink. "Good night," he said, and kissed the top of her head. "Sweet dreams."

He was at the front door when he turned and scowled at her. "Get the full story of the Deacon's House. And I'll dig into directories to track where Belknap has lived and when. Let's compare notes tomorrow by Zoom. I'm over to see Darlene and will probably be tied up until after your last class. We'll connect after that." He left.

Shanna touched her head where he had kissed her. It

felt warmer than the rest of her scalp. It wasn't like the flush she felt when they had first kissed in the car, but it made her feel good, watched over, cared for. She liked the feeling and struggled to remember when she had last felt that way.

～

Rand and Darlene were animated thumbnail images on her phone. "Been a good day," his image said. "Lots to tell you."

"And I have a lot to tell you."

"You first."

"No, you."

The frame around Darlene's image lit up. "You two can play Alphonse and Gaston if you like, but I'm going first. What we have is Professor and Mrs. Belknap living on Racine Circle until shortly before her disappearance. Then the couple moves into the Deacon's House, the lady vanishes, and the Professor's been there baching it ever since."

"Yes," Shanna said, "on rather favorable terms. He has a ninety-nine-year lease on the place, for which he paid a whopping ninety-nine dollars. You'd think the University would have tried to weasel out of the deal sometime over the last half century, but no, not even in tough times. Professor Belknap is essentially a guest of the university. Because it's university property and he is merely the lessee, under the terms of the lease, they maintain the property and provide it fully staffed and furnished."

Darlene's head was shaking. "Are you thinking what I'm thinking, Murphy?"

"I'm right behind you. What does Belknap have on the university? I'm wondering what on earth he could be holding over their heads." Murphy pointed a finger at his phone's camera. "Ball's in your court, Shanna. History. What's his story? Get on it!"

Darlene signed off, leaving Shanna and Rand facing each other's images. "I wish you were here," she said. "I'm feeling out of my depth on a rocking boat."

"Mmm." He nodded.

"Is that all you have to say? You remind me of someone I know."

"Who's that."

"A guy named David, this quiet nerd who works for a company that does research on ground-water pollution."

"Not Signachem. You wouldn't by chance be talking about the new CTO, David Jacobi?"

"Yes. How did you know?"

"Because Signachem is one of the recent trades made by Professor Belknap and by some relatives of Dr. Jacobi. I expect the feds are going to be looking into it at any moment. This thing may be escalating right out of our hands."

"I don't get it. Is David involved in insider trading?"

"Not directly, maybe, but there are people he knows who somehow knew that Signachem was about to announce a new analysis scheme and a lucrative contract with the EPA. So there's a link somewhere, including a link with Professor Belknap."

"Let me look into that link," she said. "I think I know some people I could talk with."

"Do you want to tell me?"

"Not until after a few inquiries. I'll let you know."

"Be careful."

She smiled as if he had just kissed her on the top of her head. "I will."

☙

Friday night. With the sun setting ever later, it was still bright out when Shanna arrived at the Lewises' to find the circular drive blocked by two sedans. "Shabbat shalom," Shanna said, as she edged around the cars toward Adrienne. "Which distant cousins are here tonight?"

"Shabbat shalom," Adrienne greeted her. "No cousins. My son. Rob is here with Caitlin and the twins. They flew in separately from LA, so they have two rentals. It's that West Coast jetsetter lifestyle, I guess. Mark and Rob are out back trying to wear out the boys, who are still on Pacific Coast time. Caitlin and I are catching up in the living room. I already poured you a glass of chardonnay."

Caitlin a wiry, wavy-haired woman who exuded ambition from her gold-flecked fingernails, raised her glass as Shanna entered.

"You two have met, haven't you?" Adrienne said.

"I don't think, so." Shanna accepted the glass of wine Adrienne handed her and raised it in toast toward Caitlin. "But I recognize you from your pictures."

Caitlin returned a surprised smile. "Oh, really? From where?"

"Over there." Shanna nodded toward the massive fireplace, where a gallery of family photos spanned the entire mantel. "Adrienne is such the curator of photographic art."

"Oh, I thought you might have seen the piece on me in *Film and Faction*. They did a feature—well, a fluff piece—about me as one of the, quote, new documentarians. As if I were some kid just out of film school. Hell, I've been producing and directing for more than a dozen years, with almost as many indie festival awards."

"Very impressive. Are you working on something now."

"Always working on something, but I'm not producing or directing at the moment. I'm trying to package and fund a documentary on becoming homeless, on the first weeks and months of homelessness, when ordinary families suddenly find themselves caught up in extraordinary chaos, desperately adapting to a new, harsher reality. So much has been done about the chronically homeless and little about the process of how people are pushed or tumble into it. I think my approach has a lot of potential to build sympathy, that viewers will more readily see themselves in those on-screen, rather than looking at homeless people as 'them'."

"Sounds like it could be a really important film."

"If I can ever get it made. Getting the money is the bitch, especially for indie filmmakers. That's why I'm out here. You wouldn't know anybody with a social conscience and surplus cash who you could introduce me to, would you?"

"Probably not, I'm an academic. I'm afraid I don't travel in those circles."

"Really? But you're friends with Mark and Adrienne."

Shanna and Adrienne exchanged awkward glances. "They were gracious enough to adopt me when I first showed up at Holcomb as an impoverished assistant professor."

"It's always been our pleasure," Adrienne said. "Shanna is one of the smartest people I know. Her book just won a big prize, you know."

"Oh, what is this book?"

"It's an academic study of the role of slave labor in the early days of Southern colleges and universities."

"Trendy. That definitely has some documentary potential, especially in this era of rising white guilt on the left and black dissatisfaction, well, pretty much across the board."

"I'm not sure I'd express it quite that way, but I do see a growing willingness of many Americans to come to terms with the truths about how we got to where we are today."

Caitlin set her wine glass on the glass-top coffee table and slipped an iPad from her purse. "So what is the name of your book? Any chance I could get a copy?"

Shanna told her the full title and suggested she could order it on Amazon.

"Well, I was hoping to get a signed copy direct from the distinguished author, you know."

I bet you were, Shanna thought. "I'll have to see if I have any author copies left. These academic presses are not very generous with their complimentary copies."

☙

Fascinated by the unfamiliar Friday-night ritual, Rob and Caitlin's twins quickly settled down at the dinner table. They giggled when Mark led their parents in the tradition of the priestly blessing with their hands on the boys' heads, but they clearly enjoyed it. By the time dessert rolled around, the boys were restless again, and Mark offered to teach them a new game in the living room.

With the boys gone, the conversation shifted quickly into plans, politics, and the economy. "Oh, before I forget, Mother," Rob said, "I wanted to thank you for telling me about that company that your cousin works for."

"Signachem?"

"Yeah, that's the one. I looked into the fundamentals, and it seemed fairly solid, like it might be a good addition to our portfolio, so I picked up shares and then, to my delight, it took off. Another useful tip from you."

"I'm so glad. David Jacobi is such a nice guy. And wicked smart. It's good to see him doing well. You know, he and our Shanna here hit it off pretty well."

Shanna rolled her eyes. "He drove me home a few weeks ago when he was in town. He is smart, but I don't think anything is in the cards."

"You never know, Shanna. Look at Rob and Caitlin. Who would have imagined this good Catholic girl had a Jewish soul."

"I wasn't that good a Catholic," Caitlin said, "and I can't say much about my soul."

"But you converted. And now you're raising those two wonderful Jewish boys."

"I think Rob is doing more raising than I am. He works from home while I'm on the road hustling or shooting much of the time."

"Well, Rob always was good with kids." Adrienne reached over to put her hand on Rob's arm. "He was the one, you know, who used to babysit the neighbor kids, not Maxine. I do wonder when Maxine and Harold are going to give us some more grandchildren. Not that we'd ever see them. I mean London really isn't that far, not by air these days, but do they visit? Hardly. You always were such a good boy, Rob."

Rob leaned over to Caitlin. "It never stops. Watch carefully. Study her lines. Someday, that could be you with Michael and Micah."

⁂

At the end of the evening, Rob offered to give Shanna a ride back to the University. Blocked by Caitlin's car, he backed down the circular driveway. "It was good meeting you and getting to know you, Shanna. Mom is a collector, you know, a connoisseur of character, so consider yourself among the favored."

"I do. And it was nice finally meeting you."

"Look, Caitlin is on her way up to New York next, and will have the boys with her. She wants to introduce them to Broadway, although I'm not so sure about that at this age. Anyway, I don't have to be back on any deadline. Maybe we could ... maybe we could hang out or something."

"I really don't think so."

"Don't get me wrong, here. It's not like I'm going behind Caitlin's back. We have an understanding."

Shanna tipped her head back against the headrest. "I really, really don't think so. Not judging," she said, staring at the visor. "Whatever understanding you two have is between you, but that's just not my understanding of things."

"Not judging? Really? Look, I'm not talking about some complicated deal. We spend some time together, have some fun, and no strings."

"There are always strings, not always visible, but there are always strings."

"Shanna, I really like you. Really. I think you are smart and sexy. I'm interested."

"I don't know exactly what you do in your marketing firm, but you should know, your ad copy is not selling me. Look, your mother and I are good friends, and your parents mean a lot to me. So, let's just let this one go. No hard feelings."

"No hard feelings. That's the classic line when giving a guy the shaft."

How do I get out of this, she was thinking. As he turned

into Racine Circle, Shanna was wondering just how hard it would be to extricate herself. "Nobody's giving anybody the shaft."

"Okay, okay. I get it. It's not like I'm going to force anyone. No need for that. Just, well, just don't say anything to my parents. They're, you know, not so understanding of the Hollywood lifestyle kinda thing."

"Your lifestyle is your business. If it works for both of you, then I say live and let live. Goodnight, Robert. Thanks for the lift." She stepped out of the car and closed the door with a little more force than she had intended.

Shanna made herself a cup of chamomile tea and sat at her kitchen table, staring at her phone. She knew what she wanted to do, but it was late. She tapped the number, then put the phone back down. What were they, she and Rand? What did they have?

She redialed and let it ring. She was about to give up when he answered. "Hey, Shanna. What's up? I thought you were with the Lewises tonight."

"I was. Just got back. Wanted to … I wasn't sure whether it was all right to call this late and all."

"Of course, it's okay. Anytime."

"Really? Well, I just wanted to …" What did she want? To talk? To invite him over? To talk about strings? "Oh, I have something to tell you. I think I found out the lynchpin of the insider trading business."

"Yeah?"

She said nothing for several seconds. "Now, all of a sudden, I'm not sure I want to tell you. For that matter, I can't be sure yet. Maybe I should do a little more legwork."

"I think I understand. You don't want to rat on a friend. But look, we're just investigators here, just gathering information and building a case. We're not police and certainly not judges nor juries. This is like doing history. Besides, I already figured it out, practically the moment you called."

"You did?"

"Yeah, it's the Lewises, gotta be. I know you, Shanna. I can hear what you don't say."

"I'm not sure whether that's a comfort or a worry."

"Maybe both. Now get some sleep and we'll talk more about the case tomorrow. Okay?"

"Okay. Goodnight, Rand."

"Goodnight, Shanna."

Chapter 13

Rand's voice was getting more tense by the minute. "Look, I told you there is no way we're going to get a search warrant. None of us has standing or any authority here, and even if I knew a local judge—and I don't—no judge in their right mind would grant a warrant on this gauzy story you have. It's not going to happen."

"Then we have to just go ahead and do it. That's what I did at Atlantic Methodist, basically burgled my way into the locked archives and took a lot of pictures of documents."

"You included stolen material in your book?"

"Give me credit for having a brain. And some scholarly integrity. No, I used the information to track down other sources—microfilm, personal correspondence, in one case a recorded interview in the Smithsonian archives—then collated and reconstructed the data. Everything in the book itself was obtained through proper channels, and all the citations were correct. I just left out some of the steps along the way."

"I don't know whether to admire your ingenuity or be disappointed by your flexible ethics."

"Admire both."

"You know, Shanna, the more I know about you, the messier it gets. I was intrigued by how you didn't quite belong, despite your considerable efforts to fit in. And now … it seems like beneath every layer is another layer. I figure one thing out and there's two more puzzles."

"Maybe the smart thing would be to give up. Take what's in front of you as good enough."

"I want more. I want more than good enough."

"I thought you were the one to satisfice, to settle."

"I was, until you came along."

They held each other's gaze for much too long, and Shanna was both glad there was a table between them and annoyed that it was there. She was thinking that she had already let him in too far, let him see too much. There were good reasons behind all her insurance policies, good reasons to stay protected, to stay safe.

She pushed her chair back from the table. "If you want to bail, be my guest."

"Are you talking about this case or about us."

"Take your pick."

"No, I'm not going to let you off the hook while you just accommodate to whatever happens." He looked up at her with a determined expression. "If you want me to go, just say it, but you're going to have make the choice and own it."

"How do we get from talking about cold-case forensics to … to this?"

"Because we are that, you and me. We are each a cold case, an unsolved dilemma left to grow cold, to freeze over."

"And you had to stir things up, turn up the heat."

"And you weren't watching me watching you? Isn't it

about time you were honest with yourself, at least honest enough to admit that you asked for this, you were looking for a way out—or forward."

Shanna walked over to the sink and started washing her hands for no reason at all, almost without noticing. When she looked down and saw what she was doing, she found herself suddenly at the edge of tears. "I'll do it myself. I don't need you."

"Okay. Okay and brava. Right there, you took responsibility. I'm out of here." He stood and took his sweater off the back of his chair. "But I'm not out of your life." He marched out the front door and slammed it shut behind him.

☙

It was not the first time Shanna had been in the library in the wee hours, but it was the first time in this section of the sub-basement. She placed her faculty keycard on the pad by the door, but it flashed red. She tried turning it, waving it back and forth, and pressing it against the gray surface. Red, red, red. What to do?

She found a custodian on the next corridor down. "Hi, I'm sorry, but I'm wondering if you could help me."

He leaned on his push-broom. "What?"

"I just left the Restoration Lab, but I forgot something, and now the system won't let me back in.

"Okay," he said, leaning the broom against the wall and motioning her to follow. At the entrance to the lab he held his hand out. "Let's have your keycard."

"It didn't work."

"Let me try it."

As she handed the keycard to him, she could smell alcohol on his breath. She was also wondering what it is about men that, drunk or sober, they so readily assume a woman is doing something the wrong way. She watched as the janitor tried the same variations as she had.

"Doesn't work," he said.

"Yeah, that's what I said."

"Maybe it's your keycard."

"But it worked when I went in. Maybe it's the lock."

He reached for the keycard on his belt chain and waved it at the pad, which flashed green, releasing the lock with a soft clunk. She reached past him and twisted the handle while the lock was still released. "Thanks," she said, pushing past him. He shrugged and walked away.

As soon as he was out of sight, Shanna pushed on the little button recessed in the edge of the door. The lock let out a buzz and the keypad blinked red then green, but when she closed the door it pulled open again with no resistance. "Thank you, Gareth," she said. It was a trick Professor Belknap had shown her in the early days after her arrival on campus.

The overhead lights came on automatically when she started down the corridor. She counted paces and stopped at twenty-one. If her maps and calculations were right, there should be a door right about there on her right.

"Ten feet farther." She jumped at the sound of the voice. It was Rand. "The construction doesn't match the blueprints."

"How do you know?"

"Because I checked, silly. Happens all the time. I would have thought you knew that stuff."

"I do, but … And I thought you were out?"

"Not out of your life. I still got your back. The door

should be just ahead, that is if it exists at all. My guess would be it was walled over long ago."

"Well, your guess would be wrong, because there's the door, right there." She pointed ahead.

"There's *a* door. We don't yet know if it's *the* door."

She walked past him and twisted the knob. "Locked. And it takes a real key; there's no keypad."

"No problem." Rand reached into his jacket and pulled out a keychain. "Old fashioned lock, old fashioned bump key." He sorted through the keys on the chain, tried one, then another. The third slipped in. He pulled it back out, then slammed it back in with the heel of his palm. "Didn't work. I'm out of practice." On the third try, the knob turned, and he pulled the door open.

It was a storage closet, lined with shelves stacked with cans of solvent, boxes of safety gloves, and numbered trays. A wheeled stainless-steel cart in the middle took up the remaining space. He laughed as he rolled the cart out. "So much for a secret tunnel."

"Mind if I take a look?" she said.

"Be my guest. It's just a closet."

She pushed past him into the narrow aisle formed by floor-to-ceiling steel shelving on either side. She studied those on the right, shifted some trays and boxes, then checked every shelf on the left. "Damn." She turned around. "Damn, damn, damn!" She kicked at the back wall. "What the...?" The steel-reinforced toe of her work boot had left a crater in the plasterboard. She kicked again.

"What are you doing in there? Don't wreck the place in your frustration."

She knelt down and tried to see into the darkness on

the other side of the hole in the wall. A cool, damp breeze blew in her face. "This is it, we found it, behind the back wall of the closet." She stood and started kicking at the plasterboard to enlarge the hole.

"Hold on there, Godzilla. You'll bring the night crew down on us to check out the noise."

"What are we going to do? It's on the other side of the back wall."

"My father always told me never to force entry with a battering ram when a pen knife will do. Here." He handed her a multi-tool. "Do you know how to use a Leatherman, or do you want me to show you?"

"I've used a multi-tool before."

"To cut plasterboard?"

"I can do it." She took the tool from him, opened a locking blade, and crouched down to start cutting an opening. "Oh, shit."

"Now what?"

"Nothing, just slipped."

"You sure you don't want help? I can do it, probably faster."

"Men!"

"This is not a gender thing. It's just …"

"It's never a gender thing, at least with you men. There. I think that's big enough to crawl through. If you have a flashlight, follow me."

Rand fished out his flashlight and wiggled through the opening at the back of the closet. He stood up beside Shanna. They were in a rock-reinforced tunnel facing a wall of brick. The wall was obviously old and the bricks and mortar the worse for the years. The tunnel had been bricked over long before the back wall of the closet in the remodeled library had been constructed..

"I guess that's it," she said. "We've literally hit a brick wall. So close." She stood, shivering in the damp cold, shaking her head.

He stepped over to the wall and absent-mindedly pushed on a brick. Some of the old mortar crumbled and the brick moved.

"Be careful."

"Yeah, don't worry. Just checking things out." He edged over to the side of the tunnel, inspecting the wall as he went. "I think ..." He slipped on a wet patch on the floor of the tunnel and stumbled against the wall. His shoulder sent an entire section of bricks tumbling through. Shanna grabbed his arm to pull him back even as much of the rest of the wall collapsed into a heap.

Their flashlights formed bright beams in the cloud of dust from the collapse of the wall. Shanna closed her eyes and pulled the neck of her sweatshirt up over her mouth and nose. Rand was on the ground, coughing and moaning. "Are you all right?" she said.

"I ... I think so. My leg. Some bricks." More coughing. "Let me see if I can stand."

"Here, I'll help you." She bent over and got an arm under his as he struggled to stand.

"I think I'll live," he said. "But I may have to cut back on trail running for a while."

"Here, let me take a look." She knelt beside him and worked his left pant leg up. "Ooh, ouch, that doesn't look good. We better get out of here and get you looked at."

"I've been through worse. Trust me. Besides we haven't

checked out the tunnel for what we came here for." He took a step and grimaced. "Look, why don't you reconnoiter, just past the wall, see what you can see. I'll wait here. Maybe we can sneak in again."

"You sure? You're not going to pass out on me or bleed to death or anything."

"No, you take a look around and let me lie here like a wuss."

"How do you men do that, turn hanging back into an act of bravado?"

"It's in the genome, on the Y-chromosome." He laughed and started coughing again. "Just go. Be careful."

Shanna climbed gingerly over the mound of broken bricks now half filling the tunnel. A steady rush of air blowing from deeper in the tunnel was clearing the dust. She played her flashlight beam around. There it was, at her feet. If she'd taken two more steps she would have stepped on the outstretched hand of a human skeleton. She lifted her camera on its lanyard around her neck and started snapping flash pictures from different angles. The skeleton was clean, but remnants of a calico-print dress still lay across the hips.

"What is it?" Rand's voice echoed in the long tunnel. "What did you find?"

"Abigail van der Houten Belknap."

"Don't touch anything. Those are human remains and this is now a crime scene."

"Don't worry, but I got pictures."

"I know. I saw the flash. I think we better ..."

"What?" There was no reply.

She found him unconscious where she had left him. She checked his pulse and breathing, then started strategizing how she would get him out. Or should she call for help and bring everything crashing down on both of them. She looked over at the square of light from the hacked opening in the closet wall. It would be tight, but ...

She climbed over Rand and reached through for the multi-tool. She worked quickly to double the size of the opening, then struggled to slide him closer. She crawled out first, turned around, and reached back in to start tugging him out, doing her best to cradle his head. She put her knees up, braced her feet on the wall to either side of the opening, and with his head between her legs, pulled him through up to his waist. The back of his belt was caught on the wood footing of the wall. She unbuckled the belt and tugged until it slid completely out of the loops.

A last, she had him lying on his back, out of the tunnel and partway out into the hallway. What next? She checked his pulse and breathing again. Both slow, but he was alive. How to get him out of here? She spotted the cart across the hall.

It took quite a bit of maneuvering to get his head and torso situated on the bottom shelf of the cart, with his heels dragging behind. He moaned, and she checked on him again.

"You can't just roll out of here. You have to think like a cop."

"Who said that?" Had she imagined it? Think like a cop. Blood. Prints. A hole in the wall. She went back into the closet, pulled on a pair of rubber gloves from a box, and started a hurried clean up. After the floor was clear, she stacked two large cartons to block the opening in the wall. She used paper towels to wipe everything down, made a quick check around, then closed the door and wiped the knob.

She wheeled the cart slowly back down the corridor and onto the service elevator, jamming the door before going back to reset the lock on the door to the other section.

Rand woke up when the elevator started. He started to sit up and bumped his head on the top shelf of the cart. "What the fuck?"

"Watch your head. You okay?"

"Yeah, I think so. I must have feinted. The cold, the pain, the ..."

"Don't you go passing out on me again. We're still not out of the woods."

"But this is the library."

"Well, I can see that you've recovered. Let's get you back to my place and survey the damage. I'll drive."

∾

The gash in Rand's leg was deep, and it took Shanna some time to do a decent job of cleaning and dressing the wound. "I still say we should get you to the hospital," she said. "It's been a lot of years since my first-aid training at Camp Schoharie."

"Yeah, and right down the road from the hospital is the local police station. We can save an extra trip and turn ourselves in once the docs are finished. No thank you." He pulled his pant leg down and tried to stand. "Oooh, now that really hurts. I'm going to be limping for a few days. Have to come up with a story."

"We have to tell somebody about this."

"We can't tell somebody about this without getting ourselves in a whole lot of hot water. No we have to sit on this, at least until we figure out what the next step is. In the mean-time, play it cool with the professor. We really have nothing on him, so lay off him for a while."

"I know how to play it cool. I don't need to be coached."

"Well, tonight was anything but cool. I still don't know what got into me to tag along."

"I thought you said you were watching my back. Seems yours was the back needing watching."

"Only because of you and this wild hair you got up your ass over that damn tunnel. And now we have a well-blazed trail to us just waiting for somebody to stumble onto."

"Not well-blazed. I cleaned up after us. I wiped prints, I hid the hole, I—"

"Yeah, and you left the cart taken from the storage clos-et sitting outside the service elevator. And your keycard is registered in the security system log. And that janitor who let you into the section will remember you. And ... The list goes on. You're an amateur at this, and you act on impulse."

"And you don't?"

"I don't. My moves are calculated, rational."

"Men always say that—after the fact. You didn't even have a plan."

"Men, huh? It's coming down to that time-worn trope. Men this, men that. Men always, dot dot dot. I could tell you a thing or two about women, but I'm not going to waste my time offending your feminist ears." He grabbed his jacket from the chair. "I'm going to get myself home and start con-juring up some cockamamie story for when this eventually blows up in our faces. I'll leave you to your midnight mad-ness, but count me out."

"You know where the door is. Don't slam it behind you."

Shanna started straightening up the kitchen, restoring order to her first aid kit as Rand put on his jacket and limped out in a huff.

෨

Edna Pettingale was already at her desk when Shanna arrived first thing in the morning. "Edna, what do I have to do to get a new keycard? Somebody lifted it from my purse yesterday, and I didn't discover it until now."

"Oh, that's too bad. It'll cost you $50, and you'll have to fill out a report. The people in Security don't like that, because they have to reprogram the access codes and all that. There's a form, SK-417b, not 417a, that you have to get from the faculty website and print out, then deliver the completed form to Campus Security over in the Fairlee Center, first floor of Building Two. Takes a week to ten days to get a new card. They send you email when you're supposed to come and pick it up in person. You'll need picture ID—not your keycard, of course—and a copy of your faculty appointment letter for the most recent year."

"A week to ten days? What am I supposed to do in the meantime? How do I get into my office, open classrooms? How do I even get the faculty discount in the food court?"

"Oh, that's no problem. I can give you a temporary badge." She walked over to a file cabinet, stood on tiptoe and retrieved a card from the bottom of the top drawer. She returned to her desk, swiped the card in the reader on her keyboard, and typed at lightning speed what could have been an entire paragraph. "There." She handed the card to Shanna. "That's good for thirty days, but you should be all straightened out with Campus Security long before that."

Shanna leaned over the desk and blew a kiss at Edna.

"You are a doll, a life saver, and all-around Olympic champ, Edna."

Edna grinned. "Somebody's gotta keep this place running."

≈

As Shanna headed over to her office in Stergeson, she realized she had just been given a tool. Until she actually delivered the form to Campus Security, she had two cards, one of them allegedly in the hands of a thief. It was going to be another busy night.

Chapter 14

The voice on the phone was distorted. "What the hell is going on, Shanna?"

"Well, hello Professor McMurphy." Shanna switched her phone to the other ear. "How have you been."

"I've been wondering what the hell is going on," he said, lowering his voice. "What is this shit? It's on the university website, in the Chronicle, the student newspaper. It's the talk of the town. Now they want to talk with me."

"That's understandable. Apparently, some student—or somebody—stole my keycard last week and used it to pull off something in the library. Maybe she was looking for drugs. They think the thief was female. Who knows. Anyway, the university got an anonymous tip from one of her buddies that she had found something 'really wicked cool' in a section of the library, in a closet or storage room or something like that. Now the university is forming a research team to work with the police because—guess what—they found human remains, an old body. They don't know how old, so they have called on Belknap from Anthropology, me from History, because I've studied the campus, Chriswall, our archeologist, and you as our distinguished criminologist."

"Why are you talking this way? Are you with somebody? Where are you?"

"I'm busy with a student, right now, but we can coordinate later this morning. Let's meet where we last talked. Say, noonish?"

"All right. I'll play. See you at noon."

❧

Rand was pacing in the small kitchen of her bungalow as Shanna sipped her tea. "Why didn't you check with me? Why didn't you let me know what new screwball thing you were pulling off?"

"You said you were through with me. I took you at your word. Besides, we're covered."

"Covered? What do you mean? There are log files, security camera recordings. It's not going to take a Sherlock to place us in the library that night."

"Well, now, that's funny, because whoever stole my keycard was clever and apparently used my privileged faculty access to hack into Campus Security. They were not real sophisticated hackers, but they were effective. Everything for the library for that date was wiped out before the weekly backup cycle could be completed. There's a twenty-four hour gap starting at midnight on the night of the break-in—alleged break-in."

"How the hell do you know how to hack into the security system?"

"I have many hidden talents."

"You ..."

"Me what?"

"You are so ... so clever and so infuriating."

"Back at you. I was channeling this ex-cop I know, who

134

can be an arrogant prick sometimes, but he kinda grows on you. He is so ... so clever and infuriating."

Rand looked bemused. "You're not mad at me anymore?"

"No, I'm still mad at you, and I'm not sure how much I trust you, but I think we better stick together. Otherwise, they're going to stick it to us separately." She put her hands together and looked heavenward. "Forgive me, Benjamin Franklin, for corrupting your immortal words."

∼

The first meeting of the Holcomb Tunnel Research Task Force did not start off well. Belknap led off.

"Well, we better get started. As the medical anthropologist of the group, I might as well take the lead."

"And why is that?" Jory Chriswall said. "I'm the archeologist, and this is a dig. We need to follow best practices in archeology, every step of the way."

"Jory, please. All of us respect your work, but this is not Mexico and these are not Aztec ruins."

"Well, Gareth, need I point out that we are not on some Caribbean island, either. I understand there are human remains, not a collection of tropical herbs."

"Yes, human remains. Human. I studied medicine at Johns Hopkins."

"Oh, really? I didn't know you had a medical degree. I knew you were a doctor, but I thought your PhD was in anthropology. Or am I wrong?"

"You are not wrong, but I do believe I am the senior faculty person here, with relevant expertise and a historical connection to the site."

Shanna perked up at that but said nothing.

"Historical connection? With a tunnel under the library? There is more to you than shows on your CV, then."

"I meant that the tunnel connects—allegedly—to the Deacon's House, where I have resided for decades."

"If we are going to invoke history, then maybe Professor Newsom should take the lead. Not that I'm suggesting that, although, of course, I am not objecting, either. I only ..." He trailed off and cleared his throat.

"Look, Jory, if we are going to argue relevance of discipline, history probably trumps all, especially as our own Professor Newsom has studied this very campus and even has had some connection with that tunnel."

"Well, not exactly connection," Shanna said. "I was aware that it existed based on historical documents, maps that I had seen at one point."

Rand cleared his throat. "Gentlemen, please. This is not an historical issue. It's—"

"Do you mean to exclude Professor Newsom?" Jory cut him off.

"Of course not. I just wanted to point out that we are also dealing with what might well be a crime scene, which is my field, and—"

"We don't know that," Belknap interjected. "The remains have not been identified."

"It's still a crime scene because of the illegal entry and property damage by person or persons unknown."

"I hardly see that as of much importance," Jory said, "compared to the potential significance of this discovery."

"Except to the police who are investigating the intrusion. And the university."

"Are you suggesting, McMurphy, that you should lead

our not-so-merry little band?" Jory feigned shock. "With all due respect, you're adjunct. You just arrived around here."

Belknap finally stepped in again to propose a quick show of hands whether he should continue as chairman pro tem or the group should invoke Robert's Rules and go through some kind of formal election process. Belknap graciously abstained. The vote went two-to-one, with Chriswall the naysayer. After another hour of heated discussion, it was decided that the group would convene at the site the following morning at ten.

As Rand and Shanna walked back across campus, he said, "I don't know if I have much of a future among academics. They can get so vicious over the smallest things."

"Oh, we're not so bad, as long as you stay away from committees and task forces and action groups and ... pretty much any gathering of three or more of us. I'll see you tomorrow over at the library. You think you can find the place?"

☙

The hallway was a crowd scene by the time Shanna arrived. Professors Belknap and Chriswall had each brought along two of their own student research assistants, and the Chancellor was there to oversee with her assistant.

The closet itself had been emptied but was blocked off with yellow police tape and guarded by a state trooper. The Chancellor and Professor Belknap were engaged in an agitated but low-pitched exchange. Finally, Gareth broke away from the group and approached Shanna. "What a mess," he said. "It's out of our hands. The state Division of Antiquities and Artifacts has taken over. Orders from the top down. As soon as the police are through with their job on the break-in, a team from our beloved state's flagship university will be down to study the entire site. We can, we've been told, read about it when their report comes out."

"You look upset and worried," she said.

"I am. Do we want a bunch of outsiders marching in here uninvited, taking over? Who knows what they'll do, what hasty conclusions they'll draw?"

"I would hope they are professionals and act accordingly. At least we can find out the truth of what happened to that woman."

"Woman? What makes you say that?" He frowned. "The news releases just said 'human remains' had been found, nothing about a woman."

"I don't know. I just overheard something about a skeleton of some woman."

"How interesting, Shanna. You've heard more than I have. Interesting."

෨

Shanna, Rand, and Darlene gathered at Dahlia's, which was closed on Monday's, but Darlene, never one to sleep-in on her day off, had "thrown together a little something" for lunch.

Shanna raised her wine glass. "Well, I guess this is cause to celebrate."

Darlene and Rand gave each other a look. "We're not done yet," he said to Shanna. "We haven't heard back from the state forensic lab, and that's just the start of the next phase, which could stretch out—who knows how long."

Darlene nodded. "In law enforcement, we learn not to celebrate too early. Suspects get away, perps work a plea deal, and juries can break your heart. It's not over until you hear me sing."

"And you should hear this lady sing. Sweet Jesus, can this woman belt out the good news."

"So, I take it you learned to sing in church," Shanna said.

"Bethel African-Methodist-Episcopal Church in Jamaica Plain. I was up there in the front declaring the gospel before I started kindergarten. Never stopped singing, never gave up on the Lord, but—truth to tell— I'm not sure I believe so much in His people these days. Seems to me there's just as many good and bad inside the church as outside. And don't get me started on that bunch of bible-thumping bastards up in Washington."

"I still say we should toast. Here's to all our good work on this case." Shanna raised her glass.

"And to all our good work on this next case," Rand added.

"Don't let's get ahead of ourselves," Shanna said. "As you say, we're still waiting for the lab results."

"But as you say, it looks good that we found the remains of Abigail van der Houten Belknap," he said. "In that case it's homicide, out of our hands, goes to the homicide people."

"What about the financial hanky-panky? What's your payoff?"

"Our payoff?" He spread his hand. "It's not clear that anyone did anything that rises to the level of prosecution. Belknap and Adrienne are the only ones who did anything systematic with share trading, and who's going to go after a gossip?"

"So, I guess the Carolina Troika is on furlough," Shanna said.

"Carolina Troika? What in blazes is that?"

"Us. That's the name I gave to the three of us."

"Well, this Troika is not on holiday. Darlene and I are already looking into that other cold case, another murder and money mystery."

"What's it about? Can you use an historian?"

"Maybe. This one involves an unsolved murder, mob connections, financial skimming, and a young woman who vanishes about the same time as an awful lot of money. The epicenter of all this skullduggery is your old home town, Hartford. In fact—"

"Not my home town," Shanna cut him off. "I was born and raised in Cranefield, Connecticut.

"But didn't you live and work for a while in Hartford? Maybe you even might have bumped into some of these people."

"Hardly likely," Shanna snapped. "Hartford is a big city."

"Well, yeah. Anyway, this woman might have been a victim, might even have been involved with a mob hit. Maybe a historian could help. The woman's name was Carbone, Louise Carbone."

Shanna clenched her teeth and fought to keep her stomach from rebelling.

Part 2 – Louise:

Chapter 15

She was only blocks away when she heard it, felt it, and then saw the second dark cloud rising above the buildings. The Twin Towers were gone. By now she had heard enough to know. That was it. The end of Waxman, Gold, and Walsh. The end of so many. Penny was gone. Yair was gone. And Toby. Toby Warner was dead. It was over. Everyone on those top floors—gone. A shiver coursed through her.

Out of nowhere, from the very heavens, resurrection and salvation had arrived. As she stood on the street corner, terrified and paralyzed, it fell almost at her feet. Amidst the papers and pieces of debris and half-burned bits that were best not thought about, was divine inspiration: an exit plan, a map on a small plastic rectangle.

Not everyone in Manhattan could drive, but her father, who always indulged her intellectual inclinations, had also insisted she learn three practical things: to swim, to ride a bicycle, and to drive a car. She had a driver's license, and it was current. If she acted decisively, she could get away now. If she set her feelings and fears aside and used her brains, this was not a crisis, this was opportunity. Suddenly, with planes crashing into buildings and the country attacked by an unknown enemy in an undeclared war, the rest of the country and the world had more than enough to worry about. For now, no one would pay the least attention to her.

What was needed? A quick stop at her apartment to pick up cash and a few things, then a swing into the Avis office a few blocks west before it was too late, and then across the bridge and away. Away where? Someplace where she could leave it all behind, start over, where no one knew her name or her face. As she hurried back to the apartment, she pulled out the license again. It was not a good likeness, but what license is? Look, Louise, she said to herself, there are good days and bad days, good hair days and bad. Besides, the photo was taken nearly four years ago. You were just a kid. And now? She studied the license. A few months short of twenty-four. How quickly those years passed, almost as if they had never happened. She doubled over in a fit of laughter. A man across the street, running, took no notice.

Get a grip, Louise, she told herself as she started toward the apartment. "Louise Bianca Carbone," she pronounced, speaking to the image on the license she held in front of her as though it were a hand mirror, "you are a piece of work. Whatever are you going to do, Louise Bianca? Remember, you are a Carbone, and Carbones are always … What? What are we? What do we Carbones do? We are"—she stopped for a moment— "fast thinkers, quick studies, light on our feet. What do we do? When the going gets tough, we get the fuck out of New York as fast as we can and move on. Forget what can't be changed; change what you can. Survive."

At Gordon Apartments, with its white marble facing darkened and pitted by decades of bad urban air, she buzzed to be let in and waved as she passed Mick at reception.

Glued to the little black-and-white television set behind the desk and ignoring the screens of the security cameras, he sat shaking his head and mumbling. He gave her his usual half-hearted two-finger salute without looking up. It had been the same everywhere she passed: people transfixed by a horror too strange and unexpected to be comprehended, images literally burning into the psyche on endless loops of network replay.

At the elevator bank, she pushed the polished brass call button and stood, tapping the corner of the license against the wall in an impatient pattern as the elevator car took its own sweet time to reach the ground floor. On the slow crawl up the shaft to the seventeenth floor, she shifted from foot to foot like a runner at the back of the pack, jogging in place at the start of a marathon. Once in her apartment, she saw that the maid had not been there yet. She resisted the almost overpowering urge to straighten things up and instead concentrated on scrounging what she could as efficiently as possible.

She was already thinking ahead. Eventually, somebody would enter the apartment; somebody would go through her things. She did not want to raise suspicions about missing items by taking too much or the wrong things. She skillfully triaged the contents of her dresser and threw a few necessities into her roll-aboard. "Won't be rolling that aboard any plane anytime soon," she said as she emptied the nightstand drawer of its stash of cash. She picked up her leather-bound diary, then set it back in the drawer. No mementos, no souvenirs, she told herself.

With everything given a hasty order in her suitcase and her handbag stuffed to the overflowing, she stepped out onto her balcony for a quick scan of the skyline. The air was acrid from the fires. She turned toward where the Twin Towers had been. It looked like the end of the world. In a way, it was.

At the apartment door, just before flicking the light switch, she took one last look at the luxury she was leaving. She thought of the meteoric rise that had made it possible and suddenly remembered the shoebox at the back of her closet, the first and last payout from her second job. "What an idiot you are, Louise Bianca. What was the point of the test run if you weren't prepared to use the results." She retrieved the box from its hiding place, removed the stack of banded bills, and slid it into the zipper pocket on the outside of the bag. Traveling money, she thought, something to tide you over.

That day, on her way north, she was stopped twice, but only asked for identification once. The Connecticut state trooper gave her and the license a two-second glance, then waved her through.

The first weeks in Hartford were lost in a fog of pizza and television in a cheap motel while she listened for rumblings and references that might foretell her future. In the vacuum created by a pair of hundred-story holes in space that now dominated the news and the attention of authorities, she began to put together plans. As long as she didn't do anything stupid, she could keep using the New York State driver's license, but it would be better soon to get a Connecticut replacement. She should first find an apartment, then a job, something that paid reasonably well without being too demanding, something she could fake, something with numbers. She was in survival mode, trying to think rationally, working hard to keep the night terrors at bay.

At the drugstore down the block, she bought an inexpensive diary with a little lock and key and began to tell the story of her life in Hartford, a story of becoming herself, of her search for permanence. It took her three weeks to find an apartment, two more to get hired as a bookkeeper for a small construction firm anticipating a boom in business. The job application was a five minute interview with the big boss, who spent most of the time talking about the construction business and his family. "And remember, it's not Fort Construction, it's 'FOR-tay', Italian. We don't build forts. But we are loud. Get it? Loud. Forte." Then he turned her over to Marge Caprelli, the bookkeeper who was retiring.

Marge took her under her wing and quickly trained her up. On Marge's last day, a week before Christmas, she confided in Louise. "I know. All along I know. You never did this before. You're a quick study, and you'll do all right, but you never been no bookkeeper, not until now."

"You're not going to tell Mr. Forte, are you?"

"Don't worry. And Joey don't care. Just as long as you keep the numbers straight and him out of jail, he don't care. But I do wonder where you really come from, where you were those years. What's your story?"

Louise was thinking, remembering to be fast on her feet, a Carbone. "Doing time. After I dropped out of school." That should take care of any diploma inquiries. "I drifted, did drugs, and picked the wrong boyfriend. End of story."

"Where'd you do time?"

More quick thinking as she stared at her hands. "I don't

wanna go there, not anymore. You understand. I'll do my best for Forte Construction, 'cause I don't wanna go back."

"You're not still on parole or nothin', are you? That could be a problem."

"No, I finished clean, few years back. Stayed with my parents until I couldn't stand it. Plus, they kicked me out. Now I'm starting a new life." She did a little bow and curtsy. "Louise Carbone, bookkeeper, at your service."

"Can I ask you something? You got a boyfriend now?"

"Naw, I'm done with men, least for the foreseeable. Too much trouble. You know what I mean?"

"That I do, but I still miss my Tony, bless him. Been seven years since he passed, rest his soul, but I still miss him." Her face quivered and she looked down. "But I sure don't miss his yellin' at the television"—she looked up with a twisted grin— "or his smelly socks. That man could sweat buckets into his work boots. We bought foot powder by the case. I'm serious, by the case."

Louise grinned and gave Marge a hug. "Thanks for helping me along, and thanks for keeping all this just between us."

"No problem. And if you have any problems, you can still call me. And if Joey gives you problems, you remind him that I taught you everything. Everything. And that includes how to handle the you-know-what entries. Just do as I showed you, and you won't get caught, I promise." She stopped at the door and turned back. "You look in the top left drawer of the desk and you'll find a Christmas bonus. It's the way Joey likes to do these things. He's the quiet type when it comes to the people stuff. I put in a little extra on account you're starting out and all. Merry Christmas."

"Thanks, Marge. And Merry Christmas to you. And have a Happy New Year. You've been swell."

In the desk drawer was a business envelope with "Merry Xmas" handwritten in red ink. Inside were three hundred-dollar bills. "I'll put these with my collection," Louise said to the closed door.

∾

The faith Marge had put in her began to benefit Forte Construction. Louise started doing more than just keeping the books, she started keeping watch on cash flow, controlling how subcontractors were paid, and introducing new accounting practices that made it easier for Joey to do work that looked better than it was. He was pleased and expressed his pleasure with regular raises and irregular envelopes with stacks of bills. "A little something for the long weekend," he would say. Or, "Take the day off, buy something nice. It's on me."

The long fight with the Connecticut Department of Revenue the following year put a temporary end to that, but after Joey walked out of court the last time with him and his lawyers all grinning from ear to ear, he drove straight to the office, marched in, and gave Louise a hug. "You are one amazing lady," he said. "Don't understand why there's no guy in your life. You are something."

Louise was worried that he might put the moves on her, but it never happened. Instead, she got her second raise of the year along with another fat envelope. Living alone on the cheap was working out for her. The past was past, and her tax-free savings kept growing.

∾

Jess Thibault spun like a dust-devil into her life on a Friday in mid-April the following year; by the second weekend in May, they were finishing off nearly two solid days in bed. Louise kept hearing a line from the movie "Working Girl": A head for business and a body for sin. "That's me," she said.

"What? What'd you say?"

"Nothing. Go back to sleep, Jess. I gotta take a piss and clean up or I am going to have such a UTI that not all the cranberry juice on Cape Cod will help." When she returned, Jess had taken her advice. He lay on his back, sprawled and spread-eagle, head half covered by a pillow. He was big, a massive man, who made her feel small in a way that she found exciting. He was so different from the other men in her life—the other men and boys. They had all been agile like her—soccer players, on the playing fields of the mind as well as physically—where Jess was solid, dogged, more rugby than soccer.

And here was Jess in her bed, a man who would not know soccer, mental or physical, if the ball struck him in the face. Jess did know what he wanted and when he wanted it and nearly always got it. He was Joey Forte's right hand—and his left. He made things happen in a tough, fast moving business, and he did it by being bigger and more determined than those around him—or against him.

Louise was surprised that she found him so attractive, that the physical force of his presence in the room could be such a turn on. They had flirted at the office from the moment he walked in the door, but she had managed to avoid being alone with him for weeks. Then, this last Friday, just as she was closing for the weekend, he had showed up with a dozen long-stem roses and tickets for closing night at the opera. The flowers were cliché, but the opera surprised her into thinking that this handsome hulk of a man was more cultured than he appeared.

It turned out to be an Italian illusion, arranged by the boss, who had told Jess, "If you're going to hit on my bookkeeper, you better do it in style. Here, take these. And afterwards, take her to Violetta's, tell 'em I sent you. And buy her some roses, for Christ's sake. Girls like her love roses."

She knew this, because Jess had unselfconsciously re-played the story for her, thinking she would find it amusing. She laughed, because it was his telling it that amused her.

She stayed amused until things started getting rough.

Chapter 16

Jess stormed into the little room that passed for a business office at Forte Construction, a windowed enclosure in the corner of the warehouse looking out over pallets of bricks and fork lifts and front loaders vying for space. "Anyone seen that fucker Buddy Tomasino? I'm going to kill that little cocksucker, snap his gawky little neck." His face was as red as marinara sauce, and he was panting as if he had just done a half-marathon. "He told me he was headed back here to talk to Joey. Talk to Joey? I'll talk to Joey, not that little shit. I'll do the talkin'."

Carla, who answered phones and did typing as if it were a slow dance at a high school prom, shook her head. "Haven't seen Buddy all week, Jess. Did you try Joey's office?"

"Did I try Joey's office?" he mocked her with a chipmunk voice. "Of course I tried Joey's office or I wouldn't be asking you two. Empty. What about you, doll." He turned to Louise. "You seen either of them?"

Louise, who was feeling anxious in his presence for the first time, shook her head. "I think Mr. Forte is supposed to be out at the Columbia Street site. Like Carla said, Mr. Tomasino's not been around all week. But I thought you said that he was just talking with you?"

Jess walked over to her desk in the corner and tapped so hard with his big index finger that the little desk rattled. "Don't tell me what I said. I know what I said. And I hope to fuck you ain't defending that little rat, because I don't see any future for no Tomasino. He is going down. And them Kaminski boys with him. Dumb Polaks. They'll be outa business in six months."

Jess turned out to be a fortuneteller then, and on more than one occasion in the coming months. Buddy Tomasino disappeared, and Forte Construction started a bidding war against Kaminski Brothers that was more than just about bidding.

Then Jess started showing up at the apartment late and well-lubricated.

"I don't think you should drink so much after work," Louise told him. "I worry about you driving that way."

"You worry about you, I'll take care of myself. I got a lot to deal with these days, what with the fuckin' Kaminskis and now things heating up on the other side of town. And all."

"What did you do to your face? You look like you walked into a door or something."

"Yeah, doll, that's what I did, walked into a door. Or something. Maybe a something with a Polack name." Then he did something that Louise would never have expected. He sat down on the sofa and put his face in his hands. He made no sound, but when he looked up, his eyes were wet and red.

"You wanna talk?" she said.

"No." He sat there staring into space. Louise sat down beside him and stared at a spot on the featureless wall, with a growing sense that they were both looking into the same emptiness, a void formed by losses and lost opportunities. Then he started talking.

"I was always big, you know, and that's the only way people ever saw me. It was always, you know, 'My, what a big boy you are.' And 'He's so big for his age.' It started when I was little and never stopped. Coaches saw me as a lineman, never a quarterback. Teachers put me with the dummies who struggled to read without ever asking me to read something out loud. There were the smart kids on one side and me and the smartasses on the other. If my guys ever found out that I liked to read, that when I was little I wanted to play violin, shit—that would have been the end of it." He looked at Louise, then turned back to the void. "Now, here I am, the big guy. Joey knows I'm smart, basically lets me run most projects, but I'm also the enforcer, and I don't know a way out. Basically, nobody gets out. So, I keep taking my cut and cutting off a bit more and building enough to someday buy a place big enough with a big enough fence." He threw up his hands. "Oh fuck. Why am I telling you all this?"

"Maybe because you trust me."

"Maybe I don't trust anyone, especially you. I don't know you. Hell, you don't know me." He stood up suddenly. "I need to get out, take a walk. You're right. I've had way too many shots and beer chasers tonight. Forget this. Forget I said anything."

No, she said to herself, I won't forget. And I won't let you forget.

&

It was a slow process, getting through to Jess, gaining his trust, drawing him out in those infrequent moments when, whether because he was drunk or frightened, he would say something real. The Jess who spoke to her at those times was more complicated than the Jess who took her to nice restaurants or movies or made long, slow love to her. The Jess who told her things, real things, was a tortured man who felt trapped by his size and his family, by a business that was as corrupt as it was lucrative. What he told her gave new meaning to the numbers she copied and computed in the books she kept. His stories were the stories behind the transfers and the fudging of figures, stories of greed and guile that seemed to permeate the very foundations of the buildings that Forte constructed.

Louise closed her eyes and ears to those stories as she quietly began her own construction project, putting together her way in—and her way out. She used what she was good at as she became an ever better and more creative bookkeeper. As Jess's story became more intricate, hers became more integral, more of a piece, and the entries in her diary grew shorter and more pointed. As their stories merged, she and Jess both fell into habit and repetition that lasted through the truce with the Kaminskis, more skirmishes with the tax people, and yet another year of on-again off-again border disputes with the Kaminskis.

Another Sunday afternoon, and Jess was getting ready to go, looking for his keys.

"You know, you don't have to leave," she said.

"I gotta go. I work in the morning. So do you. I'll be back Friday."

"Why not just stay, move in?"

"What, here?" He scowled as he looked around the room. "With you?"

"Why not? We've been together more than two years. Why not something beyond just weekends? We could get our own place, something bigger, nicer."

"I would think you understand. You're Catholic, you're Italian. You know how this works. It's just not done. We can't just live together, and I am sure as fuck not ready to marry you—or anybody, for that matter. Come on, doll, be realistic. We got a good thing going here. Don't I take you nice places? Don't we do things?"

Louise listened to the echoes of his words ringing in her head. A good thing going. A good thing going nowhere. There was no future for her here, no way forward, only the endless parade of debits and credits in a double-entry ledger, a life where everything had to balance out according to rules and logic that were beyond her power to alter.

Marge had been wrong. There's only so much one woman and a set of books can do. Sooner or later, she gets caught. Or the boss gets caught, which is the same thing. Or Jess. No, the only power she had was the same as Marge, the power to get out, retire early, leave it for someone else to fix up or mess up.

She was tired of being Louise Carbone, tired of the life she had slid into as an escape, a refuge. She needed something more. What did she need? What brought her joy, what gave her meaning? What was the life she wanted, not the life she had.

Louise started speculating, dreaming. Her diary entries became flights of fancy, two-column lists of plusses and minuses, short stories with happy endings. There were whole pages filled with short questions for which she had no immediate answers; there were long paragraphs struck out with scribbles; and there were entire sections recording what she was learning, what she had concluded, and what she would do next.

She took her time, spending her weekday evenings at the library, and slipping away during the day to dig into records. This time she was systematic about it, bringing to her life the same methodical determination by which she kept the books at Forte. There would be no hasty packing, no sudden exit, this time would be for good—clean and for good.

❧

Jess surprised her by moving in the next week. There was no explanation. He just showed up at the door one Monday after work with an armful of clothes on hangers, which he handed to her when she opened the door. As she held it open for him, he picked up a stack of cardboard boxes and kicked two more through from the hallway. He still had his place, which she had never seen, but more and more of his stuff started piling up in her apartment, and he was there most nights.

It slowly became clear that his idea of sharing the place was that his role was to eat and sleep there and to watch television on nights that they didn't eat out. The rest of the domestic duties were hers.

On a day when Louise had picked up groceries on her way back from work, she found Jess already sitting on the sofa. "You're early," she said, setting the two bags temporarily on the dining table. "What's up?"

"I've been reading. Interesting stuff."

"Yeah?" She moved the bags into the tiny kitchen and started unpacking.

Jess followed her. "Yeah. Interesting stuff about birth certificates and going to college and cooking the books for the mob—and against the mob."

Louise tensed. "Is this that new best seller, that thriller from—what's the guy's name, Pazulli or something?"

"No, this is by somebody named Carbone." He slammed her diary down on the counter. "Or maybe that's just her pen name."

Louise froze as she reached to put a carton of milk in the refrigerator. "I ... you have no business, no right to—"

"Who the hell are you, Louise? Who?" He grabbed her arm and whirled her around. The milk carton hit the floor and split, sending skim milk exploding everywhere. Louise tried to reach down, but Jess lifted her bodily until only her toes still touched the floor. "Who in fuck's name are you?"

"Let go of me. You're hurting my arm."

"I'll hurt a lot more than your arm if you don't start talking and making real sense."

Louise struggled to get free, but he held fast and twisted her arm cruelly. "Do you know who I am? Do you know what I do at Forte?" he said.

"You're the construction manager. You manage projects. You—"

"I'm the fucking enforcer. I put the squeeze on clients who are slow to pay. I make sure we get the best prices—one way or the other. I keep work crews on their toes and weed out the slackers." He squeezed harder. "I make people disappear if I have to. Do you understand?"

"Yes." She choked out the word. "But I thought that you—"

"You thought I what? That I cared? Of course I care. I

cared about Buddy Tomasino. We went through high school together. We were like this." He held up two fingers on his free hand. "Mongo and the Runt, they called us. None of that stopped me from doing what I had to. So start talking, doll, and make it good."

Louise reached behind her back with her free hand and felt for the big knife in the wood block by the sink. Jess had her wrist in a vise-grip before she could bring it around in front. He slammed her hand down on the edge of the counter, sending the butcher knife clattering into the dirty dishes in the sink.

"You just wrote the last page of your little diary. The last fuckin' page." He spun her around and pushed her head down onto the counter, then held both her wrists behind her back while he reached for the blender. He lowered it by the cord to the floor, put a foot on it, and yanked the cord free. He tied her hands, cinched the cord tight, and then spun her back around to face him.

"I am going to teach you a lesson you are going to remember for the rest of your short life. Then I'm going to take you to Joey, and we'll figure out what to do with our cunt accountant."

As he dragged her to the bedroom, she was wondering why she wasn't yelling for help. She should be screaming in terror. Instead, she was thinking about Joey Forte and what to do about Jess. She was back in survival mode. "Tie me up, to the bed, Jess."

"What the …? You like that stuff?"

"Do it to me good, like I deserve it. Then I'll tie you up and see how long you can stretch it out with me on top."

"You really like that stuff, huh?"

"We can take turns. Then we can see what else we might do together about other things. Remember, I keep the books. The books don't care about one account or another. One pocket is just as good as any other. Know what I mean?"

"You saying what I think you're saying? Do you know who you are talking about fucking over? This is Joey Forte. No one fucks Joey and walks away."

"Except now you know some of my little secrets. There are ways to walk away. Buddy Tomasino is not the only one who can disappear without a trace, and there's more than one kind of disappearing act."

Jess stood beside the bed, mouth open, deep in thought. The diary was fading from his memory, and he was finding it hard to remember why he had been so angry. Here in front of him was something he had never thought of before: something genuinely new in a world that held no surprises.

"We can work out the details later," she said. "Besides, it'll take months to finish setting it all up. Right now, you got me really hot with all this stuff. I want you, and I can see you want me. So let's."

As Jess untied the cord around her wrists and pushed her down onto the bed, Louise took flight. As he pounded away, she was paying fake invoices, shifting fungible assets, opening new bank accounts. As he held his hands around her throat while she pretended to climax, she was constructing a new identity for him. As he lay atop her, heavy in sleep, she twisted aside enough to be able to breathe. And to plan his death. And hers.

Chapter 17

Joey Forte showed his anger with silence and a knee that would not stop bouncing as he sat in the side chair and listened to the story spelled out slowly and in great detail, a blitz of numbers with too many digits. "And you're sure about this?" he said.

"I'm sure." This was how Jess had wanted it. She had rehearsed her lines while he had blocked his own scene. "None of these companies are real. All of these checks were deposited to the same two bank accounts, and according to East Hartford Commercial Bank, they were both opened by Jess. He's been playing you. He tricked you into approving the payments."

"What took you so long, if it's that bad?"

"I'm just the bookkeeper. I keep the books, pay the bills, make the deposits. I do what Marge taught me and what you and Jess and Carmine tell me to do. If it's got your initials on it, I pay it. But when this here payment came in, I thought it was a deposit on a new contract. It bounces, and I started digging. It clears on the second try, but then I started wondering about what the project was and what these charges were for. And I didn't want to say anything until I was sure.

Absolutely. You understand. And I knew you would want to see it all laid out for you, so you'd know it was real."

"Yeah. But it's Jess, my cousin's kid we're talking about. Course, she married that Frenchman, Thibault. You can't trust the French. Jess has got that Frog blood in him. I shoulda known."

"What's going to happen to him?"

"That's my worry, not yours. Keep this between us for now. Don't say a word to Carla. She'll blab."

"Maybe he can pay it back."

"Yeah, maybe he can pay it back—in blood. Nobody fucks with Joey Forte."

Louise could feel her heart speed up. It was all coming to a head. Was everything in place? Had she forgotten anything? Would Jess be able to pull off his presto change-o? She put her fist to her mouth as Joey stood to leave.

"Don't you worry. Just keep doing your job, and everything will be fine. I'm going to get my wife's cousin to come in and take a look at the books, just to be sure about all this. He's an accountant, big corporate stuff. He'll know what's really going on."

At the door, he stopped before leaving. "Understand, it's not personal, Louise. It's not that I don't trust you, but Jess is family, even if he's half Frog. And you're just you. But we'll get this sorted out, and then we can all move on. Right from the beginning, I told you I'd take care of you. Joey Forte takes care of his people, one way or another."

Louise watched him as he left the warehouse. After making one last entry in both sets of books, she left to make a stop at the bank before heading for her apartment.

࿔

After one body was discovered, the initial headlines were sensational, but it was a team of investigative reporters who broke the full story several months later.

Bodies, Bogus Books, and Building Trades Warfare

It was a small packing crate, and Jessup Anthony Thibault was a big man. Some creative effort had been required to fit the body into the limited space, then to slip the heavy package onto the worksite where the new Blanchford Plaza was under construction by Kominski Brothers Builders. It took neither creativity nor effort to notice the smell.

And how did the body of Thibault, a trusted employee of rival firm Forte Construction, end up at a Kominski site? That's the question that continues to plague Hartford Detective Arthur Landsdown and his fellow officers and that this newspaper has been investigating for the last four months.

According to Joseph "Joey" Forte, president and CEO of Forte Construction, the Kaminskis had Thibault killed as a threat and out of revenge for what the Kaminskis were claiming were unfair competitive practices.

According to Jan Kaminski, head of Kaminski Brothers, Thibault was killed because he was stealing from Forte with the help of his girlfriend, the bookkeeper for Forte. The body had been planted at the Kaminski worksite to frame them, Kaminski alleges. It was all part and parcel to a panoply of improper and illegal practices by Forte and his firm, including but not limited to shakedowns, bribery, theft, stealing customers, and sabotaging construction sites.

Two days after the discovery of Thibault's body, police found an abandoned vehicle with bloodstains type-matched to Thibault and a woman's purse that includes the driver's license of Louse Carbone. From evidence found in the car, police believe she, too, was killed, but as of this writing, her body has not been found.

Because the bookkeeper had been involved with Thibault and was among those last seen with him, Forte's company books were subpoenaed and found to contain irregularities, including nearly $3.5 million in funds not accounted for. Forte, himself under suspicion, pointed the finger at Thibault and Carbone for "rippin' him off."

What your I-Team reporters have uncovered may be even more complicated.

Part 3 – Darlene:
Chapter 18

The dining room
at Dahlia's was silent except for the muffled sounds of back-of-the-house staff working in the kitchen and empty except for the three of them at a corner table. The dateline on the printout of the newspaper story resting on the table was nearly eight years earlier. Shanna Newsom could read the boldface headline, which danced in her vision as she fought against panic. Darlene looked over at her. "You all right, girl. You look like you seen a ghost or something. Maybe one that don't smell so good."

"No. I just get, like, these spasms sometimes. Got a touchy stomach. Rand can verify."

"You know, I got something for that. Let me mix up this little tonic I know. Very soothing and settling."

"Thanks, but I think I'll be fine. Just need a minute or two."

Darlene nodded, but her expression was still a question mark. "So, you knew this Carbone woman, did you?"

"No. Like I said, Hartford's not a half-horse town like Taggertsville."

"Just wondering, because it seems you were living in Hartford about the same time as the story broke about

Louise Carbone. It was after you finished at that defunct university up in Vermont."

"Kennilwirth wasn't defunct when I got my degree."

"No, course not. What about when you were in Hartford, the big building trades scandal? You don't remember. You were there about then."

"Was I?"

"Yeah, at least that's what it said in your application for a copy of your birth certificate from Connecticut Vital Records."

"You've been stalking me, too?"

"Nobody's stalking you. Rand and I just always do our due diligence. Just comes with the ex-cop territory. Right, Rand?"

Rand's chin bobbed. "Just old habits, like I told you, Shanna."

"Well, I'm not so sure I like some of your old habits." She turned to Darlene. "Or yours."

"Chill, girl. We're all friends here. Just thought you might already know about this story. It was pretty big news in Hartford at the time. Here,"—she held out a stapled stack of paper— "here's a printout of the whole series, 'Bodies, Bogus Books, and Building Trades Warfare.' Some headline, huh? You can study up on it. We thought we'd do some more work on the case while we're waiting for the lab results on the skeleton in Holcomb's closet."

Shanna took it and set it on the table after glancing at the first page. "You know, I'm really not feeling so good. I probably should head back to the house."

Rand pushed his chair back from the table. "I'll drive you back."

"No, don't bother. I'll use the Uber app. You guys enjoy the rest of your lunch, and don't worry about me. I'll see you tomorrow, Rand."

"Don't be silly. I'll drive you."

Darlene put her hand on his arm. "Let the girl do what the girl wants to do. You don't always have to play the first responder, you know."

Shanna retrieved her purse from under her chair. "Thanks, Darlene. We'll be in touch."

Darlene waited as Shanna walked to the front of the restaurant and thumb-typed on her phone before walking out the door. Rand was eyeing Darlene as she stretched her neck to see out through the front windows. "And what was that about?" he said.

"What do you mean?"

"You kinda leaning on Shanna, then edging her out on her own."

"No such thing. I was just leaning on you, my macho boy scout, always stepping in to help. The girl can make her own way home."

"Come on, maybe you fool others, but you can't pull the wool over me."

"Well, let's just say maybe you and me need to talk some more about your girlfriend."

"Not girlfriend."

"And now who's failing to fool who?"

"Just say what you were going to say about that whole performance you just pulled."

"Okay, I confess. I was testing her, seeing if I could get a reaction without revealing too much."

"This is starting to sound serious."

"Starting for you, but I'm way ahead. Look at this." From inside her chef's jacket, she pulled two pages of screenshots and spread them out in front of him. "This,"—she pointed to an entry on the one screenshot— "is the line, number fourteen, from Connecticut DPH Vital Records database showing her application for two copies of her birth certificate. And this"—she pointed to the other sheet— "is her taking out a library card a few weeks later. What do you notice?"

"Well, that she used a wallet copy of the certificate as ID to obtain the library card."

"What else?"

"They give the same address: 1756 Runyan, apartment 3B. So? Of course they'd be the same. What do you expect?"

"Yes, of course, but why would they be the same as this?" She flipped through the printout of the newspaper article that Shanna had forgotten to take. "There, read that."

"Okay. 'Police searched the alleged victim's last known address, an apartment on Runyan, but reportedly found nothing of use.' So what? Shanna and this victim lived in the same neighborhood."

"No, they lived in the same apartment. I checked an old city directory for Louise Carbone, the alleged victim: apartment 3B, 1756 Runyan."

"Okay, what's the bottom line?"

"Three-point-five million dollars, nearly. Two dead, missing millions, and a roommate."

"But wouldn't the police have looked into that?"

"Maybe they didn't know there was a roommate," Darlene said. "But it gets even more interesting if you broaden your search from Hartford and corrupt construction companies. Which I did." She smiled, waiting for a reaction.

"Okay, I'll play along. What did you find in your brilliantly broadened search?"

"You know, there are some names that you have no hope of tracking down with online searches. I grew up with a girl named Sue Smith. Don't expect to track her down on Google with a name like that. But if you know she was Suzzana Melodie Smith, you have some chance of finding out what happened to her."

"What happened?"

"To Carbone?"

"No, Smith."

"Oh, she married this jerk, Teddy Braunwain, had three kids, divorced and remarried and … never mind. Back to our Louise. If you Google Louise Carbone, you get maybe five thousand hits, but type Louise Bianca Carbone, in quotes, and the search is considerably narrowed."

"Like how narrow?"

"Other than those referring to that Hartford lady, only a handful pop up, all of them references to a woman in New York."

"What about the woman?"

"She disappeared, presumed dead, on or about September 11, 2001. She worked in the North Tower, in a restaurant."

"Windows on the World?"

"Yup. Only somehow she lived on and moved to Hartford and got messed up in some nasty, expensive business with mob-infested builders."

"And you think Shanna knows something about this Carbone woman."

"I'd bet my restaurant on it." She pushed her bulk up from the chair and stood beside Rand. "I hope I don't have to tell you to play it cool with your friend."

"Yes, cool. But maybe not my friend after all." Disappointment and resignation began to color his face.

Chapter 19

Shanna sat at her vinyl-covered kitchen table staring out the back window above the sink and nursing a mug of tea that was getting cold. The trees, now fully leafed-out, filled the view out the window, but Shanna's mind was not on her surroundings.

What to do about Darlene, that was the question. Was there anything to be done? Was it back to square one, with a quick exit and disappearing act the only way forward. That would not be forward; it would be a giant step back, back into the shadows.

What terrible dumb luck it was that Darlene had moved down here to open her restaurant and had ultimately dragged in Rand to pursue a cold case, a wild goose chase involving Professor Belknap. Unfortunately, they brought baggage with them. They brought Louise Carbone along, and now Louise was here, a ghost, an uninvited guest for dinner. Or was it for a funeral?

Shanna cradled the mug without drinking the tea. She remembered Louise. She could picture her, with her long, nearly black hair, her preference for lipstick in dark shades, and for loose-fitting clothes that she somehow thought made her look less conspicuous. She remembered the diligence with which Louise worked, the careful, methodical way she went about daily life, careful until she got involved with the wrong guy. What made women do that sometimes?

There, she thought, that's the way we do it to ourselves, as if it were a female thing, picking the wrong friend, the wrong lover. "It's a people thing," she said, talking to the tea. "Men make mistakes, too. They're just better at blaming others when they do. We women take it on ourselves, turn a miscall into a character trait, and conclude there is something wrong with us, that we're the ones who are flawed, that we will never get it right."

Louise Carbone did that too. According to the story, she fell in with that mob guy and got them both killed. Or maybe he fell in with her and got them both killed. Funny how it could be said either way, but the first way just comes so ready to mind and seems so much easier to say.

It was all stereotypes, she acknowledged. Men were this, women that. But stereotypes arose from some soil, some ground truth that could be—and had been many times—confirmed by numbers. It was certainly true in the data of Shanna's life. And Louise's.

What else did she remember about Louise? It would be easier if she had notes, something written, but now it was just whatever she still carried in her head. The overlap in Hartford had been brief. Weeks? Months? How had they met, how did they know each other?

She held the mug near her lips without actually drinking, her breath and voice making ripples on the surface. "You need to remember this stuff if you're going to be able to deal with Darlene—and Rand. It would be easier if you knew what they know."

What was in the records, out there, suspended in the Internet? There was one way to find out. Darlene wasn't the only one who could do online research. Besides, historians approached these things differently, looked at resources differently, followed different lines of connection. Maybe she had an advantage, even if they were two to her one.

Start with the newspaper article. Oops, left that at the restaurant. Oh, well, easily retrieved online. Time to find out what happened, what the rest of the Louise Carbone story is about. And the early chapters. Who was Louise before she arrived in Hartford? Why have I never done that bit of digging? Why have I been so reluctant to fill in that part of the picture?

Shanna shoved her cold tea in the microwave, tapped for a one-minute blast, and left to boot up her computer and start learning about Louise Carbone. Quickly lost in links and databases, newspaper articles and official records, she didn't hear the microwave beep when the tea was hot or when it beeped again—and again. She almost didn't hear her phone.

"It's me." The voice sounded almost sad.

"What do you want, Rand?"

"Well, a sweet hello to you, too. How are you feeling? How's the tummy?"

"Okay. I said I'd be fine. Where are you?"

"I'm still at the restaurant with Darlene. We just got some news I thought you might be interested in."

"Yeah? What's it about?"

"Our cold case."

Shanna was thinking, oh no, here it comes, get ready to

run. "So, what's the news?"

"The preliminary forensic report came back on the remains in the tunnel. They're older than we thought, early twentieth century, believed to be the body of a young woman who may have been killed in the tunnel. So, a murdered woman, but not Abigail Belknap. Another mystery added to the stack, but this one is for the historians and the forensic archeologists."

"I guess that settles it. I was so sure we had found Abigail. I should have recognized right away that the remains were too old to be Abigail's."

"That's what happens when we become wedded to one hypothesis. We see what fits and are oblivious to what doesn't."

"And what's your hypothesis? What are you wedded to?"

"I'm with Darlene, who still thinks Belknap is our man, but I don't think we are going to just stumble on a body that nobody else has ever found. So, o historian extraordinaire, what else have you dug up about the professor?"

"Nothing new. I got distracted by your other cold case, the mob story from Hartford. You know how it is. You get caught in click-throughs and scrolling and sidebars."

"Yeah, I know. So what did you find out about that Carbone woman?"

"Well, I found out that I do know her. Did. Sort of." She paused to organize her thoughts. "There was this woman who I contacted through the Kennilwirth alumni association when I was briefly down in Hartford, digging into old records. I needed a mailing address in Connecticut to have some documents sent, so she said sure, I could have mail sent to her address and she'd hold it for me. I only met her when I picked up the mail. I can picture her—vaguely—and I had misremembered her name. I thought it was something like Carmini, Lois Carmini. Like I said, I only met her that one time and it wasn't all that big a deal. I never connected that with the mob story because, around the time that story broke, I was too heads-down into my historical research to pay much attention to current events. So mystery solved."

"Yeah, I guess. Mystery solved. Or one small piece of one mystery. There always seem to be another layer underneath. In any case, I'm still pursuing the Belknap mystery. I'll leave the Hartford case to Darlene. Keep me posted on what you learn about the professor."

☙

The kitchen at Dahlia's was noisy and busy. Darlene was at the two-top over to one side, catching a hurried early bite before the dinner crowd swept in. "Grab a seat. Want a bite?"

Rand shook his head but sat down. "You said you had something you wanted to tell me in person. So, I came back. You know, I do have a day job, and I have a class that I have to prep for."

"Well, here's the deal. I decided to check Shanna's story about the Carbone woman being an alum of that college, uh, Kennilwirth University. What you told me."

"And, let me guess, you didn't find her?"

"You're right, I didn't find her. And I didn't find our Shanna Newsom either."

Rand was open-mouthed. "So neither of them? They're not in the Kennilwirth records?"

"No, they're not. For that matter, nobody is. There are no records."

"You mean Kennilwirth isn't real?"

"Didn't say that. Kennilwirth was real enough, plenty of proof of that, but there are no student records, no alumni lists, no databases, no nothing. When this for-profit education conglomerate, NovaDidaxic, killed it, they killed it good. Anything they couldn't sell ended up in a landfill, which includes all the paper records and old disks and back-up tapes. Nobody was watching, nobody thinking. The archives, everything, gone."

"Wow, what a tragedy."

"Or what a convenience? An educational history that nobody can check. And a perfect explanation for why no one can check it. The records were lost, obliterated in a corporate blunder. Or plunder."

"But that doesn't mean Shanna did anything wrong. She could just be another victim, one of many former Kennilwirth students. This doesn't mean her PhD is not legitimate. I mean, she has a publication record, and it was good enough for her to get hired by Holcomb."

"Whoop-de-do. You were hired by Holcomb, and you have a correspondence course master's in criminal justice and no publications that I know of."

"It wasn't a correspondence course. The program mixed residential study with remote learning. Besides, Shanna was hired into a tenure-track position; I'm adjunct faculty. Hell, even you could teach adjunct at Holcomb if you wanted to."

"Touché. I might even actually consider that someday. It don't look like it, but this restaurant business is taxing, and I'm not talking about the IRS. But, back to Professor Newsom. According to the Wikipedia entry for Kennilwirth, the year she lists for earning her PhD happens to be the first year Kennilwirth had authority to grant doctorates, which also happens to be the last year of its existence."

"Again, maybe more coincidence."

"More convenient coincidence. But wait, there's still more. In all the world, there appears to be only one academic in any field who lists among their qualifications that they received their doctorate from Kennilwirth. One can find a few dozen who proudly proclaim master's degrees from Kennilwirth, but Shanna is the only doctoral laureate—if we take her word for it."

"You don't have to take her word for it. I've seen the diploma. It's real, in a nice frame on the wall in her office at Holcomb, right beside her master's and an acrylic plaque, the award for her book. No, I'm telling you, it's all real. She's real."

"You are wedded to your hypothesis, Randall. Could it be your personal involvement is clouding your ability to weigh the evidence?"

He faced his palms up and shifted them up and down alternately as if weighing a couple of melons at the grocery store. "Hmm, seems like circumstantial evidence and not very weighty."

"Maybe you're using the wrong scales. We're looking for leads, not a grand jury conviction."

"Not we. You are the one looking for leads on an old murder case in Connecticut. I'm looking for leads on a case down here."

"There's over three million dollars missing in the Hartford case. I would think that would be a fair amount of incentive for you."

"Mob money. Nobody in their right mind goes after that."

"The bookkeeper was bonded. The company had fraud coverage. Recover the money or some part of it and the insurers will pay a percentage. Think with your mercenary mind, not your hormones."

"Not fair. And not true. Actually, you were right before. My personal involvement is clouding my judgement, only the clouds are thicker and darker than I was ready to admit."

"Poor boy. You may be in for a sudden thunder storm."

"Enough word play for the day." Rand felt his phone vibrate in his pocket. He pulled it out. "It's a text from Shanna: 'Got something very interesting. Swing by house tonight.' Well, curiouser and curiouser."

"You going?"

"Why not?"

"You want backup?"

"Are you serious? We're talking about our quiet, well-behaved professor."

"Or maybe we're talking about somebody who helped whack a mob enforcer and his girlfriend and has been on the run for years. I'll be on call. Just send a blank text if you need me."

Chapter 20

Rand stood on the front step of Shanna's place, his hand poised to knock. "I thought I heard you drive up a while back," Shanna said, as she opened the door. "How long have you been standing there?"

"Not long. I was sitting in my car for a few minutes. Thinking."

"Well come do your thinking over a cup of hot tea. How about a change of pace? I just made a pot of Earl Grey. Don't you love the scent of bergamot?"

"Mmm, does smell good."

"Guess where I was this afternoon," she said, as she led the way to the kitchen.

"Digging in more tunnels?"

"No, I was at an all-faculty gathering hosted by no less than the Chancellor himself and the Dean of our School." She poured two cups of the fragrant brew. "It was a farewell toast, champagne and all, for our dear Professor Belknap, who has just officially announced his retirement at the end of the spring semester. So, we have less than two months to finish our work before he's off to Italy."

"And that's a surprise?"

"A little one, since he wasn't slated to finish until the end of the year, after teaching one more course in the fall semester. I think he has been reading the handwriting on the walls of tunnels and is deciding to exit early, before his past catches up with him. This is one cold case that may be about to get even colder."

"Mmm."

"That's all you have to say?"

"Thinking. If he really is getting antsy, then we want to keep a close watch on him, track his moves. Maybe you should cozy up a bit to the gentleman."

"Yeah, I was thinking that, too. And my records research did turn up a bit more about the Deacon's House. It's care, in perpetuity, is covered by a special endowment that was funded shortly before the Belknap's moved in, which was just after it had been fully renovated to the tune of the mid six figures.

"Fairlee money?"

"I don't think so. I'm still digging. But the timing seems significant."

"Timing is always significant. *Post hoc, ergo propter hoc.*"

"You like quoting that, but you do know it's a fallacy, one of the classic fallacies of reasoning. Just because something comes later, doesn't mean it was caused by the earlier something."

"Yeah, I know that," he said. "Sometimes a thing appears to have happened earlier, but it's an illusion, a mere shadow cast later."

"Now you're talking riddles."

"I'm in a riddle mood. People are riddles. All of us."

Shanna covered her rising anxiety with another sip of tea. "You think so?"

"Always. We're always more than we appear to be. Who can ever know? Can one person ever truly know another?"

"Maybe not, but maybe that's not necessary. Maybe enough is good enough. Do we know somebody enough to trust them, to trust that the unknown, whatever it might be, is something you can deal with?"

"Now who's talking riddles?" he said.

"You said people are riddles. We're people. How much do we trust each other? Enough to trust in the unknown, to let the unknown be whatever it is?"

"Let sleeping dogs lie. Is that what you're saying?"

"Maybe the dogs are not real, or maybe they're cats."

"Now you lost me completely, Shanna. We've gone from riddles to rabbit holes and through the looking glass."

"Okay. Are you going to tell me why you're here?"

"Because you had something to tell me. In person, not over the phone."

"Right, I said I had something to tell you. Not over the phone, and not while you were at Dahlia's."

It was Rand's turn to take on a defensive posture. "What does Dahlia's have to do with it?"

"It's quite a classy restaurant. Ever wonder about that?"

"Darlene worked hard to put that together, to build it up."

"And where did the money come from to buy it in the first place? Just the down payment was quite a piece of change."

Rand fidgeted in his chair. "I don't know, her savings, I assume."

"Her savings from being a cop and then from working in the restaurant business after she finished at the Culinary Institute of America?"

"Right."

"The CIA in Boston is quite the prestigious school, and not cheap."

His growing irritation was impossible to miss. "Where is this going, Shanna?"

Where is it going? she was thinking. Turn-around is fair play. The best defense is a good offense. What's sauce for the goose. "Real estate transfers are public records, you know. Of course you know that; you're in criminal justice. And you would certainly know that Randall Sean McMurphy is listed as a co-owner of Dahlia's Restaurant."

"It's just … it was a formality, to help her get the mortgage. A single Black woman from out of state, I mean, the banks around here are not exactly colorblind, despite the laws and the claims to the contrary."

"So they listened to you, a single-white male from out of state who had been working two low-pay jobs and studying criminal justice at night school?"

He looked as if he were challenging her, daring her. "Well, it helped, obviously."

"Obviously. And we know why, don't we. Which one of us is going to say it, Rand? It's a matter of public record. Who talks first?"

He sat in silence, teeth clenched.

"Money talks. Isn't that right, Rand? In this case it was your money that talked."

He held himself rigid, saying nothing.

"You better start talking, Rand, or this is over. And

maybe a lot of other things are over, too."

He stood slowly and crossed to the sink with his tea. He set it down gently. "No," he said, and walked out the front door without saying another word.

It was Shanna's turn to sit in silence, stunned by a riddle. What had just happened? She didn't know whether to feel relieved that she had deflected a mortal blow or to be devastated by a tragic loss.

Chapter 21

Darlene's apartment was almost as small as Rand's, but hers was full of well-tended plants, the walls were hung with watercolor art, and the furniture looked as if it had recently been delivered. "I just got home, Rand. It was a long and busy shift. This better be important."

"She knows."

"Everything?"

"Probably not, but enough."

"Is she going to bring it down?"

"I don't know. I don't think so. It's like a détente. Or a cold war. Move and countermove, but nobody pushes the big red button because then everybody loses."

"All right, then it's obvious what we do."

"To you maybe, but I don't know what we do."

"We drop the Hartford project. Let it be whatever it is. Nobody up there is pursuing it, and we don't even know enough to know where it might lead. The whole thing with Shanna might be irrelevant. Maybe her dark backstory is something else altogether."

"Do we sign some sort of arms limitation agreement or

just pretend like the missiles don't exist?"

"Can we work with her on the professor? If she's game to play along, it buys time and keeps all parties occupied. And, who knows, we might resolve the mystery, maybe even make some money."

"I suppose it's worth a try." The skepticism in his voice was sharp-edged.

"Look, here's another thought. If she already knows, maybe the best ploy is to come clean. That way we get her back on the same side and rebuild something like trust. And maybe things work out for you after all."

"You are something else, Darlene."

"You bet. Now go get some sleep and let me get mine. We got some busy times ahead." She stood and reached down for his hand. "I love you, Randi."

"And I love you. Even when you call me Randi."

Rand was waiting under the carport when Shanna came around the back of the house to retrieve her bike in the morning. His clothes looked as if he had slept in them, and his face was shadowed by dark whiskers. "Let's talk," he said.

"My turn to say no. You had your turn last night. Now I need to get to the office."

"The office can wait. We can't."

"There's that royal we again. Maybe there was a 'we' at one point, or at least the potential, but not now. That ended last night." She strapped on her bike helmet and slipped her briefcase into the pannier packs slung over the back wheel. "I'm off. See you in class, Professor McMurphy." She stepped into the bike and put her foot on the pedal.

Rand grabbed the handlebar, stopping her from leaving. "Okay, don't talk. But then finish the job yourself. You're an economic historian; do your research. Follow the money trail, check the numbers, see how they add up. Then, when you think you have filled out the spreadsheet, come back to me and ask me about the missing cells. This time I'll say yes." He let go of the bike and stepped back.

Shanna was nonplussed. "Okay. I'll do just that, but you better be sure that's what you want, everything spread out and spelled out."

"That's what I want. I'm through satisficing." He looked her straight in the eyes. "I want it all." He turned and started walking back down the block to where he'd left his car.

☙

The day tumbled by like a barrel caroming down a rock-strewn slope. Between meetings with students that she cut short and a class that she finished ten minutes early and a lunch that she wolfed down without even tasting it, she snuck back into the office to pound the keyboard and fist-pump as she smiled at screens that finally made sense. She was on a roll, sucking down a firehose of findings.

As she approached the faculty garage to pick up her bicycle, Gareth Belknap hailed her. "My dear Professor Newsom," he said, "do wait up. You are much too fast for an old man."

"Oh, I'm sorry, Gareth. What can I do for you."

"You can grant me the pleasure of your company at dinner next Thursday. I realize there are diminishing opportunities for a reprise on our pleasant evening of some weeks ago. Do say yes."

"Yes. I would be delighted. Thank you for inviting me back."

"My pleasure, entirely. And consider the invitation to include a 'plus one' should you wish to bring a gentleman friend."

"Very sweet of you, but it will probably be just me. I'll let you know, either way."

"Either way, then. I look forward to much good conversation." He bowed ever so slightly and walked away.

Shanna headed for Stergeson before remembering that she was actually on her way home. She fetched the Cannondale and raced back to Racine Circle. There were files on her computer that she wanted to check against what she had discovered during the day. Follow the money trail, he said, read the numbers. It had been good advice, and most of all, it meant that Rand had intended her to find out. That was not just writing on the wall, that was a full-color animated billboard by the highway. She was almost embarrassed at how excited she was as she approached the bungalow.

There was a silver and black state police car parked in front of the house.

Chapter 22

"Ma'am, are you Professor Shanna Newsom?" the trooper asked, as he approached.

As she walked her bike up to the house and tucked it under the carport, Shanna took a deep breath. "Yes, I am. What is it, officer?"

"Do you know a Randall McMurphy?"

The buzzing in her ears was getting louder by the second. "Yes. Why?"

"We found your business card in his wallet. There's been an ... an accident. We didn't know who to notify. We thought you might ..."

☙

At County General, she thanked the officers for the ride and strode through the big automatic doors to face the reception desk. "I'm here to see about a patient, Randall McMurphy. Is he all right."

"And your name is what?"

"Shanna Newsom."

"And what's your relationship with the patient?"

"I'm ... I'm his sister. Newsom is my married name."

"Ah, yes, here it is. He should be coming out of surgery about now. Check in at the nurses' station on the third floor. The elevators are straight ahead and to the left."

∾

They were wheeling the gurney down the hall when she arrived. "What happened?" she said as she walked alongside. "Are you all right?"

"Nothing to worry about, ol' pardner. It's just a flesh wound."

"What?"

"I don't think you're supposed to be talking to me." He nodded toward the policeman standing outside the room they were approaching. "I've got a lawyer on the way. Some guy Darlene called."

"Are you in trouble?"

"Depends on your definition. Interfering with an officer in the line of duty, resisting arrest, impersonating an officer, assaulting an officer … I forget the rest of what the bozo beat cop listed as he read me the riot act. Of course, most of those charges will never stand, and a smart DA will drop them, but this is Taggert County, and who said the county DA is smart." He got a dirty look from the cop at the door but ignored it as he continued talking while the nurse and an aid helped him into the bed. "They have to make a lot of noise in a case like this to cover their dirty asses. Nothing like a bad call on an officer-involved shooting to make a cop look real bad, as I should know, if you recall. And then mix in the whole racial issue and—ooh boy—you got one real mess in the making."

"What did you do?"

"I told you, but I probably should shut up until the lawyer shows up. Oh, look who's here. Hi, darling Darlene. For-give me if I don't stand. They did a rush job patching up my leg, and I'm still a little funny from the stuff they shot me up with for the surgery."

Darlene pushed past to the bed and took his hand. The policeman who was now standing in the doorway said, "I wouldn't if—"

"I wouldn't if what, Julio. You know who's on the way? Terrell 'T-for-Trouble' Blackstone, Attorney-at-Law. You re-member him, Julio, right? Seems like he reamed you and your partner good after that high-speed chase incident."

"Look, Darlene," Julio said, "I'm just doing my job, guarding the perp, ah, I mean the suspect. Whatever."

"Then get your Latino ass out that door and guard, dammit. And leave us to ourselves here."

Officer Julio Arnez sheepishly stepped out of the room as Rand started to laugh, almost hysterically. "Not exactly procedure, Officer Darlene, but bee-you-tee-full effective."

"You ain't seen nothing until you watch Terrell at work. These guys hate him because he is one badass lawyer. Ex-pensive but worth it."

Darlene proved right. Terrell was a handsome Black man in a white suit and an attitude, who arrived with a writ in hand and an order to have his client transferred, at county expense, to Mercy, the private hospital in Taggertsville. Rand, who was still recovering from the effects of the anes-thetic asked him why. "Because it's closer to where you live and it will be cheaper to get home when they discharge you in a day or two. Besides, it lets them know who's in charge."

"I take it that's you."

"You bet your sweet ass. Now fill me in. Darlene only

gave me the Marvel comics version on the way over."

As they waited for the ambulance that would make the transfer, Rand started telling his story. "I'm at my car in the grocery store parking lot, about to slip a bag of groceries and a six-pack into the trunk, when this Black kid, maybe fourteen or fifteen, comes running tear ass right toward me diagonally across the parking lot with this look on his face I can only describe as smug fear. Just then, a foot patrolman rounds the corner of the building, running as fast as his tummy tire will allow. He stops, pulls his piece, and takes aim. I drop my stuff in the trunk, stick my hands in the air as I step away from the car, and shout, 'Don't shoot! I'm a police officer.' The idiot leans to the side and fires. I mean, there's civilians in the lot, some ducking down behind their cars, some standing around, confused, and this complete clown fires. He's shooting at the back of an unarmed kid running away. But he's such a fail that he misses and hits me in the leg instead. I'm down. He runs straight after the kid, who is now almost to the edge of the lot that abutts Hambley Park. The cop has his piece out in front of him like he was going to try to get off another round on the run. Idiot! As he runs past me, I spin my bleeding leg around, and he face-plants right onto the asphalt. Broke his bloody nose. He's reaching around, fumbling for his piece, which went flying when he went down. I swear, the guy was ready to blow me away, except by now we're surrounded by people with their smartphones out, recording or live-streaming the whole thing. I mean, Taggertsville is majority minority, and I don't think there was a white face behind any of those phones."

Rand paused to take several breaths. "The cop looks around and suddenly he's all procedure, by the book. He cuffs me and Mirandizes me and calls for an ambulance and squad car. By that time, the kid was probably across the park and halfway to the next town. This cop is pissed, I mean red-in-the-face pissed. He accidentally lets me slip as he's helping me to my feet. Now why is he doing that anyway? I mean, I'm bleeding like everything, and this guy helps me up and then let's me hit the pavement again. I'm in cuffs, I hit my head and wake up in the ambulance on the way here."

"Is that it?"

"Pretty much. Oh, I overheard. They're gonna claim the kid assaulted an officer."

"Did he?"

"Maybe, if you count spitting at the cops feet, which is what the clown cop tells his buddy. Stupid ass move by the kid, yes. Death penalty offence, no."

"Was the police officer white?"

"There's only two non-white cops in Taggertsville, and Julio standing right outside is one of them. I think the other one is at the edge of town with a radar gun, at least that's where I usually see him. So, yes, the officer involved was Caucasian, if memory serves."

Terrell started ticking off questions. "And you stepped into the line of fire?"

"Yeah."

"It was unintentional, right?"

"No, I wasn't going to let another Black kid get shot like that."

"Another?"

"Just an expression."

"So, you're really a cop? Off duty?"

"Way off duty. I'm an ex-cop. From Boston, in case you

haven't figured out the accent by now."

"And that's what you said. Or meant to say, except for the stress of the situation and all. Okay, enough for today. Not a word to anybody without me being there. So let's make sure you and me both got this right. When you suddenly realized somebody was pointing a gun at you, you inadvertently stepped the wrong way, into the line of fire. And, in a moment of panic, you said cop instead of ex-cop. Very understandable. Then the officer somehow tripped over you, probably because he was focused on the fleeing boy." He put away his pen. "I think we got this. Yeah, we got this."

"Are you telling me to lie to a jury?"

"Hardly. That would be subornation of perjury. I'm just making sure I heard you right. And who said anything about a jury? This is never going to trial, although that would be fun. These boys are going to let go of this like it was a potato that rolled right out of the fire. These boys still don't know what to do with a Black dude out of Yale Law who knows how to play the games they've been playing in their all-white league ever since Reconstruction."

As they wheeled Rand out of the room for the transfer to Mercy, Shanna realized she was seeing him in new light. She beamed him an approving smile.

"Back at you, Professor," he said. "I'll see you in class."

While waiting for Darlene to swing around with her car for a lift back to campus, Shanna scrolled through her contacts and tapped on a recent addition. "Hello, Aretha Barley? Hi, it's me, Shanna Newsom. From Holcomb. Remember? Have I got a story for you."

❧

When Mercy Hospital discharged Rand two days later, he

was walking with a cane and with some difficulty. Darlene rolled her eyes, and Shanna gave him a look laced with disapproval. "Is there an elevator in your building?" Shanna asked him.

"This is Taggertsville, not Manhattan. I doubt there's a building in the entire town that has an elevator."

"Mercy Hospital," she said. "They didn't just roll you down the stairwell in that wheel chair."

"Doesn't count. Technically, we're in Brownsdell Township. Anyway, my apartment's a third-floor walk-up."

Darlene shook her head. "No way you going to manage that."

"Are you challenging me?"

"No, just calling it like it is. Look, you're staying with me."

"When did your place get an elevator?"

"Well, but it's only one flight up."

"I wonder." Shanna frowned and looked to the side, deep in thought. "You know, you could stay at my place."

"Uh, really? I heard it's kinda small," Darlene said. "How many bedrooms you got?"

"Two. But one is my office, and ... No, Rand can have the bedroom. I can sleep on the sofa. It folds out. I'll be fine. This way he doesn't have to climb stairs and he's only a few steps from the university."

"More than a few," he said.

"Okay. Okay, we retrieve your car. Then it's a two minute drive. Easy." Shanna grinned, obviously pleased with herself.

"Easy for you to say, not so easy for me to do. My leg is so stiff and sore that I can barely manage getting into a car, much less driving it."

"I can swing by and run you back and forth," Darlene said.

"You have a restaurant to run," he said. "And it's on the other side of town. I think—"

"Hey," Shanna interrupted, "I can drive you."

"I thought you couldn't drive," he said.

"I didn't say that. I said I didn't drive. Different."

"Okay, I suppose. But I hate to put you out this way, especially with all the recent … well … stuff between us."

"We can talk about that later. I think we are going to have lots of time to talk. And plenty to talk about."

"Speaking of talk," he said, "Holcomb is a small community, one that is, frankly, still under the influence of its biblical roots in many ways. There'll be talk, all right."

Darlene nodded. "He's right, girl."

"Not until and unless they know."

"Oh, they'll know, all right—fifteen minutes after they notice that my car has been parked out front of your place all night," he said. "Maybe twenty minutes, tops. Be realistic, Shanna."

"Does that bother you? I mean, if people talk."

"No, not really, but I hate to see your reputation sullied."

Shanna gave him a crooked smile at the thought of what rumors might spread around campus. "I'm not worried. I think I know how to handle it. I'll tell Edna where you're staying while you're recovering, then the word will get around all the faster."

Darlene looked puzzled. "And that's better?"

"Yes, because if it comes from Edna, people will assume

it's all right and proper, with the official Holcomb University imprimatur. And she'll get the story right, without embellishment or poetic license."

Chapter 23

Neither Rand nor Shanna were ready for the response from the Black and Hispanic communities in the coming days. Black students stopped him on campus to shake his hand. The local Spanish-language cable outlet interviewed him, and after the Chronicle story hit, the city papers sent reporters—Black reporters.

"You're a hero," she said, as she pulled his Civic to a stop under the carport at her place. "Face it. You redeemed yourself."

"Redeemed myself? For what?"

"For that Black kid in Manhattan."

"If you think what happened here has anything to do with what happened there, you're wrong. He's still dead, and it's still my fault, and neither of those things is ever going to change."

"Tell me that history wasn't on your mind when you put down your groceries and stepped in front of that bullet."

"It wasn't on my mind. There was nothing on my mind. I just did what I did. Period."

"And what about Darlene? Nothing on your mind there,

too? You just did what you did."

"I don't think you know what you're talking about. If you mean that time during boot camp, I—"

"I'm not talking about that. I'm talking about what happened after, about what you did afterwards."

Without replying, Rand opened the passenger door and struggled to get out of the car.

"Hey, let me help."

"I don't need any help, and I don't need your approval, especially when you don't know what you are talking about." He slammed the car door and limped around to the front door of the house and stood on the step. "You got the key, or did you lose your keys again?"

She caught up with him and opened the door. He pushed in ahead of her. "I'm tired. I'm tired of limping around with a cane, I'm tired of mooching off of you, and I'm tired of everybody thinking they've figured me out, when nobody knows. Nobody." He maneuvered past the still-open sleep sofa and went into the bedroom. He was in the process of closing the door when Shanna blocked the way.

"Maybe I don't know you, not all of you, but I think I know enough. I know about you and Darlene and what you did."

"I told you. The restaurant was no big deal. I just co-signed for her. It's just paperwork, no big deal."

"What about Jamal?"

Rand painfully seated himself on the edge of the bed and looked up at her. "How? How did you …?"

"I did what you told me to do. I followed the money trail, I dug into old records—not just yours—and I started to get to know Randall Sean McMurphy. That's how I know."

He kept looking at her, blinking away tears, but saying nothing.

"Darlene had a son. You had a son," she said.

"Yeah." He let out the breath he was holding. "One time, just that one crazy time in the back of that van. That's all it takes, right? We knew we were all wrong for each other, even as we fucked our brains out. Then we find out she's pregnant. By the time we came to terms with the fact that we weren't going to make it as a couple, it was too late to have an abortion. Besides, I think she really wanted to have a kid, like she had this story in her head, about being a Black cop, a single mom, raising a kid right. Darlene was never one to settle. If she couldn't have a husband, she would have everything else. You can see what she does with that restaurant: nothing halfway about that, nothing halfway about her."

"So you supported her."

"I did more than that. I had a son. Do you know what that means to a man, to a man who is prepared to be one? I grew up trying to be a son to my father while he was too busy being a cop to be a father to me. Hell, he wasn't even a father to my brothers. He was a drill sergeant, an instructor at the police academy. None of the three of us ever had any choice about becoming cops. He wasn't raising sons, he was raising recruits. I was determined to do better. I tried." He put his head in his hands and started sobbing silently.

Shanna waited for it to pass before sitting down beside him. She placed a hand on his leg and sat without moving.

"He was a beautiful baby. I was over there so much, I probably changed more diapers than Darlene did. I bought him stuff, took him to the playground, walked him to school the first day of kindergarten, and listened to him talk about the white boys after and ... Jamal was like a philosopher, an anthropologist, right from the start. He talked with me about the kids at school and how he thought people worked. After the start of first grade, he came home one day with this poem written in crooked block letters. He called it 'Kids at School'. It was simple, almost silly, but it was eight words packed with more insight than you expect from a seven-year-old.

> Ugly, cute.
> Pretty, plain.
> Faces, stories.
> Different, same.

"By the second grade he was writing these poems that could wrench your gut and make you angry or sad—or feel like maybe there was hope for the human race. This one he wrote over the summer called 'Chalk Lines' I loved so much that I memorized it.

> I think lots.
> I think in squares.
> Sidewalk chalk lines hold my thoughts.
> Hopscotch in the air.
> Can I cross those lines I draw?

And then he started the third grade and then he was dead." Rand shook his head. "Senseless. If I had been a believer, I would have said goodbye to God right then and there that day. I was on my way over, to take him and Darlene to a baseball game down in Pawtucket—big deal for all three of us. Traffic was—well, it was Boston in the summer—and I was late, too late. I should have been there already. Maybe I could have ..." He fell silent.

"What happened?"

"You didn't find the story? I thought you were this hot-shot historical researcher. It was in the Boston papers."

"I found one of the stories, didn't say much."

"It was a drive-by, had nothing to do with him. Three tough teens in a car aiming for a gang member they thought had betrayed them. They were poor shots and driving too fast. A little girl lost her arm and Jamal lost his life. Senseless. Another Black kid is killed and somehow it's my fault. I took it on. Only that time, that time I joined the department's gang unit, determined to track down the kids who killed him."

"Did you?"

"No, you hardly ever get those guys. And when you do, you find out most of them are really not that much different from the ones they killed. It makes no sense, but it's real. Circumstance. Chance. If the traffic had been lighter, maybe I would have been there when they drove by. Maybe I could have drawn my piece from the shoulder holster—I'd made detective, and I always carried when I was off duty—and maybe I could have gotten off a couple shots before they turned the corner. And maybe there would have been another dead teenager, maybe along with some old lady carrying groceries who gets slammed into a tree when the wounded driver loses control. I don't know, but whenever I replay those old tapes, I always end up feeling somehow responsible." He wiped his eyes on his sleeve. "Darlene is always teasing me about being such a boy scout. I was never in the scouts, but something in that mindset got imprinted on my brain. That's the real reason I'm here. Holcomb is a place I can start making a difference, giving something to these kids who are first in their families to go to college. I know I'm the old white guy looking out at these scattered black and brown and yellow faces, at the occasional turban and the couple of young women in headscarves, but you know what else? I know I'm finally doing something good with my life."

"But why Holcomb?"

"Good god, Shanna, isn't it obvious. This is the only place that would have me. Besides, Darlene was here, and I still feel—always will—that I owe her something."

"You owe her? Isn't it the other way around?"

"Hardly. I owe my life to her. She helped me get sober, steered me back to school, dragged me down here to apply for an adjunct position. No, she doesn't owe me anything."

"What about the money? You said follow the money trail, but it only goes so far. Some of the cells in the spreadsheet have blank values."

"You really want to know? Remember what I told you about Pedro, Darlene's ex. Remember, what I told him? Never ask a question that you don't want to hear the answer to. Are you sure you want to ask this question?"

She took his hand. "I'm sure. I want to hear the answer, whatever it is."

He took a deep breath. "Okay, here goes. Manhattan, September 13, 2001. I'm in uniform, I duck under the yellow tape, and go back to the alleyway where I spotted that kid. I dig where he was digging, and there it is, nearly a hundred thousand in neat little bank-taped packets, bundled with wire. The kid had already grabbed the purse when he came across the cash. He was stuffing what he could in the purse when I spotted him. He was leading me away from it by running, probably thinking maybe he could come back later. There was no lady who had stuffed her purse with hundreds. They were from some delivery or bank transfer or something. Not like anything I'd seen before, so I figured it was mob money, or at least non-kosher. You know what I mean?"

She was not looking at him. "I think I know what you mean. I know a little about that kind of money."

"Yeah, well, the kid only had the woman's handbag. I came equipped with an expandable backpack, which I got back through the police line by slipping an evidence tag on it."

"So that's where it all came from. It was your money, stolen money, that financed the restaurant."

"Stolen money. Found money. Nuanced terms, Shanna. Anyway, it wasn't my money that financed the restaurant, it was hers. I used the cash to set up a trust fund for Jamal. She thought it was an insurance payout after my dad died. When Jamal was killed, the trust fund went to her. She was always good with money. She made good investments and parlayed it into enough to put herself through the CIA and to buy into a couple of Boston places and finally to own her own place, Dahlia's."

"Does she know the real story, where it came from?"

"No. I never told anybody. I was too ashamed. And too proud. I had to bite my tongue more than once. I'd managed this coup. I was Robin Hood. I had taken dirty money from the wealthy and laundered it and given it to this poor Black kid and his mom. But I don't think the law would have seen it that way. So,"—he held out his fists, wrists together— "my life's in your hands. The cuffs are in my back pocket."

Shanna laughed with her nose dribbling and tears steaking her cheeks. "Thank you. Thank you for trusting me."

"I do. The cuffs are in my back pocket."

"For real?"

"Scout's honor." He held up two fingers. "Not sure how the boys do it. I never was a scout, too busy ducking my dad's training programs. I always carry a set of cuffs with me, and I keep a loaded semi-automatic locked in my glove box. Perfectly legal, but I have these old habits, as I keep telling you."

"You keep telling me, but something's not right. The sequence. Your story, some things don't fit in time. I thought you quit the force after New York. Now you are saying you took the money and set up a trust fund for Jamal, but you were still a cop when he was killed. What came first, what next?"

"It's that *post hoc* thing again, and you wanting to figure out the because. Sometimes time is more elastic than we think, sometimes in the retelling or the rethinking we get the order wrong but the connection is still right. I quit the force because of what happened in New York, ultimately, but I quit the force after Jamal was killed, after I couldn't save him and I couldn't get the guys who did him. I quit after my failures became total, complete, after I had everything, absolutely everything I needed to end it all. So I did. I ended it."

He swiveled toward her. "Now it's your turn."

"Not yet. There's something else I need to learn about you first." She gently pushed him back onto the bed and started unzipping his pants. She gave them a tug. "I don't think you'll be needing the cuffs tonight."

Chapter 24

Shanna was awakened by the sunlight streaming in through the window at the foot of the bed. She twisted onto her side and found Rand already awake, watching her, smiling. "What took you so long, sleepy head?" he said.

"Dreaming. I had the sweetest dream about you and me. And you in me, and on me, and under me. If I told you the whole dream, I'd run out of prepositions."

"Funny, I had a dream something like that, only I'd run out of positions."

"You mean prepositions."

"No, positions. I had no idea there were so many."

"Well, we did have to improvise a bit last night, given your leg and all." She ran her hand slowly down his belly. "Did we forget any? Is that the position you're taking today?" She gave his penis a squeeze.

"Upright and ready, that's my position. It's a new day, and we haven't made love yet."

"Hold that thought. I need to pee and then I need some tea."

"Oh, good idea. How about that good stuff—what is

it?—the Earl Grey."

"Oh please, not first thing in the morning. English Breakfast Tea or nothing."

"Okay, not first thing. First thing we make love, then we have some Earl Grey."

"No, first I pee, then we make love, and then we—"

"Make love again." He pulled her over on top of him.

"I have to shut off the alarm first."

"I don't hear an alarm."

She pried his arms free and slipped out of the bed. "The bladder alarm, dear boy, the bladder alarm." She trotted to the bathroom.

಄

It was nearly nine o'clock when they finally sat down with a pot of tea. Over her protests, he'd made Earl Grey. "My father would never have forgiven you," she said. "Earl Grey is an afternoon tea. He was British and very particular about his teas. Very particular about most things, not the least his daughter."

"Mmm. Tee or thee—afternoon, morning, in bed, on the floor—whatever you say, wherever you say, whenever you say."

"My, you are the appreciative one."

"I told you, I'm fed up with satisficing. I want it all."

"Well, we will have to stop to eat sometime. Man does not live by bed alone."

"Groan. Terrible. Are you always this silly after …?"

"I don't know. It's been so long I don't remember. Maybe I was silly back then, but I don't think so."

"What do you think? What are your thoughts? I want to hear. I want to hear it all. You promised to tell me."

"I promised nothing."

"Last night. You said we had to do something first, then you'd tell me. You promised."

"There you go, editing the past again. Keep it up, and I'll have to start distrusting you. Patience, love, patience and trust. Today I have prep and classes in the afternoon. And tonight I have dinner with Professor Belknap."

"What? You never said anything."

"Well, I was going to tell you, but somewhere along the way I was rather interrupted by you getting shot. But, you know, this could work out. Belknap said I could bring a friend and hinted that might be you. Maybe he was ahead of us. Here we are, a couple, and we can go as a couple tonight."

"We can go as a couple tonight, and you can stall all morning if you want to, but I'm not settling. I want to know you, about you. I told you my secrets, things I've never told anyone. I want to know yours. Like, what is the mystery about Louise Carbone? What is your connection to her? Who is she to you?"

"She is me."

"What?"

"I'm Louise Carbone. At least I was, for a time. You thought your story was dark and complicated? Wait until you hear mine."

"I'm waiting. Tell me about Louise."

Shanna looked at her watch. "Okay, but first I have to tell you about somebody else."

Part 4 – Toby:

Chapter 25

Toby Warner was not quite twenty and already on top of the world. Literally. From her outside table in a restaurant atop the World Trade Center, she looked out over the Manhattan skyline and took another bite of her Tournedos Rossini and another sip of the vintage burgundy she couldn't pronounce and another look at Felix, the devilishly handsome and embarrassingly wealthy founder and CEO of Scaled Simulations, Inc.

"I wish we could do this sort of thing more often," she said.

"You know we can't. If my wife figured out, it would ..."

"Yeah, I know. Just wishing." She stared past him out the window again. "Oh, look, a shooting star."

"I don't think so," he said without turning to look. "Just a plane coming into Newark, I'm sure." It was vintage Felix, correcting her with sublime confidence, even in the absence of information.

"No,"—she stood her ground— "it was a shooting star."

"Meteor. They're not stars." More correction.

"I know." She lowered her voice to just above a whisper. "Star light, star bright, first star I see tonight. I wish I may, I wish I might, have the wish I wish tonight."

Felix laughed. "You can be such a naïf. And so sophisticated and so … so very, very sexy."

"You left out brilliant. You liked that math I worked out for you, didn't you?" she said, eager for his validation.

"I loved it. It's a brilliant solution, good stats, good economics. You pulled the macro and the micro levels into one clean model. I loved it."

Toby loved it too. She loved being told she was beautiful, sexy, and brilliant by the men in her life. Felix topped the list of men, and that was more by age than stature. That, too, was a big part of the excitement, that a man nearly twenty years her senior could meet her as an equal—in bed and on the mental playing fields of high finance where they had met. The two of them played intellectual soccer, running their ideas past each other, shooting for goal, playing for advantage in relentless-paced dialogue that was as exciting to her as the sex. The sex was the best she had known, and she understood the ingredients that made it so potent. He was skilled, so tuned into her and her needs, in part because of his age and experience, and she was so exciting, so electrifying to him, in part because of her youth and inexperience. It was new for her, and that made it new for him.

And it was doomed, not so much for the age difference but because of the life difference, a difference in portfolios. Felix had investments. He was married, with three kids, two houses, a yacht, and properties all over Manhattan and in Aruba. She was a prodigy with no property and no strings, a kid just starting out but already flying high and on target for a sail into the sunset.

She knew exactly what she was doing, or at least she had convinced herself of that. Felix was there for her, but only on his own schedule, just like her always-busy father had been. Years of therapy had deprived her of the ability to kid herself about how much she was acting out her childhood traumas and triumphs. Growing up, she had two loves: math and soccer. She was only really good at one, but they both gave her the joy and validation she never got from her father.

What if her mother had lived? That was a question that haunted her, and she had written pages of fantasies in her diary that explored one scenario or another. But Stella had not lived. She had died—by her own hand—when Toby was only five, leaving Toby in the hands of a taciturn father who knew nothing about children and very little about human beings in general, which always struck Toby as odd, considering that people were his livelihood, that some of his work as a photojournalist had won awards for its empathic portrayals of people in crises. But Wallace Warner saw his subjects as patterns of light and dark, shapes and shadows. His real work was in the darkroom, where he became a magician with emulsions and light. When he was not out on assignment, he was in the darkroom that had once been the master bathroom in their New York City condominium. He was, for much of her growing up, in the next room but miles away from her, hiding behind his red light, protected behind his fog of chemicals.

Toby had early figured out that there were other men in the world. Her uncle was the first to bring the light of affection and attention into her life. Simon taught her how to dribble and shepherd a soccer ball, how to set up a shot on goal, and how to mislead an opposing player by feinting one way while sending the shot another. It was an on-field skill that she carried into the rest of her life and would practice for the rest of her life.

Her uncle's accessibility and gentle coaching filled her heart with love until he remarried and moved to Florida. It was his gentle coaching when he returned for an extended visit after her bat mitzvah that was her first introduction to the thrills and terrors of sex. In therapy, she had learned to call it by its right name. It was assault, child abuse, but at thirteen it had been something else, both frightening and exhilarating, like the roller coaster at Coney Island. With Simon, who was probably more scared than she, it had never progressed beyond touching, but it had whet her appetite.

With the second man in her life, she was the coach, leading the way for Will Cantry to a first attempt at penetration, a failed attempt that had left Will humiliated and her unsatisfied.

Did any of that count, she wondered. They were just boys, even her uncle, who was boyishly aggressive on the soccer field and ultimately much the same in her bedroom, where he acted more like a teenager than even Will Cantry had.

And there was Eli. She could hardly leave out Eli, who was a boy when they married and still was when they separated a year into the mistake. He still was convinced they would get back together, that she was going through a phase, a passing diversion to be outgrown. They had met in college, playing intramural soccer, both too busy to go out for varsity, but both too absorbed in the game to sit on the sidelines. He, too, was older, already a sophomore when she was admitted as a sixteen-year-old quirky prodigy. By her junior year, with Eli approaching graduation, separation loomed on the horizon. The proposal came after a weekend match as they walked back to the Bunkhouse, the two-bedroom walkup Eli shared with three other Columbia students.

"I got a job," she said. "I've decided to drop out. I say, screw this academic bullshit. These people—Waxman, Gold, and Walsh— are ready to pay me six figures to do it all for real." She stepped ahead and turned to face him. "So, do you want to get married?"

"Uh, wow."

"I'll take that as a yes. Let's celebrate our engagement by getting a hotel room for the night. Would you like that?"

"Wow!"

It was Eli's watchword. He was the Wow-Sir, as he was known to his roomies. Sex with Eli started out awkward and stayed that way almost until the end. His marriage to her had been, without his knowing it, an own-goal by the goalkeeper, the deciding point in his losing the match that ultimately cost him the title.

The shift from a collegiate playing field to the big leagues of Waxman, Gold, and Walsh had been both easy and hard. Intellectually, it was like coming off the highest slide at a water park: effortless, thrilling, terrifying. It was like good sex, only in digits and data. She quickly realized she was the smartest person in her department, and she was soon taking the lead in building new mathematical models and improving old ones.

Socially, the entire scene was far more awkward than either she or her employers had anticipated. She was the kid in the room, the adolescent at a party for the middle-aged, the center of attention, put on display but clearly not part of the scene. She could not even drink. Not legally.

Felix Halberg, whose company was being considered for possible acquisition, had been the lone ranger coming to her rescue. When Waxman, Gold launched a joint project with Scaled Simulations, Felix had asked for her by name to join the project team. Was his interest for her brains or her body? She didn't care. Within weeks of splitting her time between floors at the World Trade Center, he was hitting on her and she was loving it.

When she worked out that he was cheating on the contract with Waxman, Gold and cheating on his wife with his secretary, Toby put herself in line for the roller coaster. It worked. He dropped the late twenties secretary for the teenage wunderkind and initiated Toby into new ways to make love and new ways to make money in the world of finance.

As had been true for her from elementary school through college, she was soon the student outshining her teachers. She found ways to put together things from Scaled and things from Waxman to make computer algorithms that worked better than anything either company had. Of course, she wasn't supposed to be doing it, so she set up dummy accounts to enable her to start running model-driven trades on her own. She shuttled client funds in and out as needed, covered trades with creative accounting, and watched the numbers climb. And climb.

She was well on her way to being wealthy before her twenty-first birthday. She only needed to work out a way to get the money out and convert onscreen digits to in-the-bank dollars. A cultivated friendship with Penny Stanfeld in the transfers department taught her about wire transfers and interbank money movement. She started flirting with

Yair Staltzman, a near-sighted specialist in European operations with a Jew-fro the size of a weather balloon. She began to complain of glitches with her computer terminal that gave her excuses to hang out with the crew in IT tech support. Her maneuvers were not about those people or about relationships; it was all just numbers and instructions and puzzles to solve. She loved it.

Then Mo Gold, scion of the original Hyam Gold who had been a founding partner of the firm, called her into his office.

Chapter 26

Mo Gold might have been fifty or he might have been much older. Toby wasn't sure. She knew she wasn't very good at pegging the age of older people. Anyone over forty was just "older." He was dressed in what she thought of as "bankers' attire": three-piece pinstripe suit with a subdued polka-dot tie.

"You wanted to see me?" she said.

"Yes, please come in, Toby, and close the door behind you. Is it all right if I call you Toby?"

"Sure. It's my name."

"What does it stand for? Tobiah?"

"No, it's just Toby, not a nickname. I guess my mother liked the sound of it. Or something." She sat down in the arm chair facing the desk and squirmed as she tried to get comfortable. "She used to tease me when I was little by calling me The Question. You know, 'Toby or not Toby, that is the question.' Uh, sorry. Free association. I do that when I'm a little nervous. Like now. What is it that you wanted to see me about?"

"I wanted to see you, uh, Toby, about some—what shall we say?— irregularities in your division."

Toby tried to put on her cool face, the face her uncle had taught her, the unreadable one that kept opposing players guessing which way the ball might be going. "Irregularities? What do you mean?"

"It appears that somebody in your division may have been diverting company and client funds for unauthorized trading."

"Ah, I wouldn't … I didn't …"

"Look, everyone agrees, you are have one of the brightest minds in the company. At your age, even. Amazing. Which is why I'm talking with you. Whoever has been doing this is really bright, cleverly covering their tracks, or at least most of them. You see where I'm going with this?"

Toby tried to slow her breathing. "Ah, maybe."

"I have a question for you, then, which I want you to think about carefully before you answer."

Toby tried to sustain the cool face, but her jaw was beginning to ache and a tremor was starting in her cheek. "Okay," she said. The shake in her voice startled her.

"So, Toby, will you take charge of the internal investigation?" He leaned forward expectantly.

"What!?"

"It's a big responsibility, and you will have to work with the utmost discretion, but I want you to turn your skills to the task of discovering the extent of the deception and to expose the culprit. Are you willing to do that? Can you do that?"

"I … I don't know, sir. It's … it sounds complicated."

"I realize that, and I do want you to work with our information technology security team and with standards-and-practices, but I want you to be our lead detective, as it were, at least initially. If the other guys, the big guns, come in too fast, I'm afraid we might lose the chance to catch the culprit and recover all the assets. You understand?"

"Yes, I think I do." She started to relax, but her mind was racing ahead. "So, you want me to work quietly but quickly."

"Yes. Can you do that?"

"Yes. I'll get right on it." She started to push up from the chair. "Can you give me any more details. I mean, what exactly is this person doing?"

"That's what I'm depending on you to find out, and I don't want to skew your investigation. Start where you think it makes sense and go wherever things take you. You're the genius; I'm just an old stockbroker at heart. And not a word to anybody at this point," he said, "not even the people in security or in standards-and-practices. You report to me directly, and you work alone for now."

"Right. I'll do that. I'll let you know when I find something." She stood.

"No, I want you to let me know everything you are doing. I want daily reports. I'll have my secretary put you into my calendar and send you an internal email with the times."

"Uh, sure. I mean, certainly. I'll do that."

"I expect you to start immediately. This very afternoon. This is a pressing matter of utmost importance to the firm. And not a word to anyone."

Toby left. I just dodged a bullet, she thought. Now I just need to figure out how the hell to string the old man along while I clean up my mess and get my night work wrapped up.

She kept up the cool face most of the afternoon as she

pretended to be doing her regular work. Behind the cool face she was working out the end-game strategy while beneath her fingers she was quietly beginning to cover her tracks. It was almost six when she made her discovery. She wasn't the only one shuffling accounts at Waxman, Gold, and Walsh. She was, in fact, a bottom-feeding fish in a tank full of top predators.

શ્

She was heading for the elevators at the end of the day when she spotted Felix studiously scanning the closing market results on the big wall displays in the hallway. "What brings you up to our floor, uh, Mr. Halberg?"

"You," he said quietly. "Ellen has, on impulse the origins of which I cannot fathom, taken the kids to Florida, a surprise visit to her mother. I thought we might seize the day and spend the night?"

"Your place or mine?"

"Mine? Are you crazy? We have a concierge, security cameras—and servants. No, I was thinking of your place. I've never seen it. We could order in, have the whole night …"

"Yeah, that could be good," she said with smug smile. "A nice finish to a good day. Do you know the address?"

"I know. I have access to personnel files. I'll see you at eight." He gave her a wink and headed away from the elevators.

As she rode the local elevator down to transfer to the express elevator on the 78th floor, she was thinking it was shaping up into a real red-letter day.

શ્

Felix arrived at the apartment a little after eight with takeout sushi from the Japanese restaurant down the block, along with a tall slim bottle of wine in a paper sack. "Everybody does chardonnay with sushi, these days," he said, "but this guy I know who works at Windows on the World says a dry Riesling, like one from the Alsace, is a better match."

"Sounds yummy."

"Yummy." He laughed. "That's you. Yummy. And so articulate."

Toby pouted.

"There, just what I'm talking about. You can be so smart and sophisticated one minute, and the next ..."

"Fuck you, old man. Speaking of which, you want to fuck first or after we eat?"

"Both. I'll put the sushi and the wine in the fridge. Point the way. And holler from the bedroom when you are ready after trying on this." He pulled a two-piece bit of lace and fluff from his inside jacket pocket. "French, straight from Paris, picked it up myself last week. None of that catalog stuff for you."

Toby held it up for inspection. "Might be a bit small."

"Skimpy can be good. Go put it on so we can start with hors d'oeuvres."

"What's on the menu?" she said, coyly.

"Wait and see, love. Wait and see."

Once the lingerie was displayed and dispensed with, the lovemaking was fast and to the point. The dinner after was an all-you-can eat seafood smorgasbord. Felix had bought enough for a family of five, which was what he was used to doing. When they drained the last of the Riesling, Toby retrieved a half-finished bottle of a white blend from the back of her refrigerator. At the sight of the supermarket bottle, Felix expressed his disappointment. "What, no sauvignon blanc?"

"No, just blank de blanc." She wove her way back to the dining table and set the bottle down in front of him.

"Cute. Multilingual nonsense."

"Not nonsense. Parse it. Fill in the blank."

"Are you always so analytical, so clever to a fault."

"Always, more than you think." She wanted to tell him about what she had pulled off at work, what she was pulling off two floors above him at the office. Would he be appalled? Or proud? Not yet, no, not yet. Maybe after she finished the job.

"Speaking of clever," he said. "You know what I heard on the grapevine today? Waxman, Gold has problems."

"Really, I thought we were as solid as bullion. Our market cap is way up since our last quarterly report."

"Not the kind of problems I'm talking about. What I heard is that they have some dumbass who thinks he's clever pulling a fast one on the computer-driven trading, except their security people have these checks and flags that spotted something going on. They let him go long enough to be certain, and now they've set a trap. They're recording everything he does."

Toby choked and coughed. "That wasabi. That's really hot."

"Just the way I like it. Here, have another swallow of your blank white wine." He poured some more in her glass. "That should help."

Nothing was going to help. She was going to jail. Nineteen years old and on her way to prison. Did she have enough on what those at the top were doing to bargain her way out? Probably not, not yet. She chugged the last of her wine. Might as well make the most of the last night of freedom, she was thinking.

࿔

Their second round of lovemaking took on a certain desperation that made it harder for her to climax. In the end, they slithered away from each other and slept sweating on opposite edges of the bed. She was awakened by the sound of the shower. Felix emerged from the bathroom wearing her flower-print robe. "I borrowed some of your shampoo, too. Sorry. Sorry to wake you, but I have to get to the office early. I have an eight o'clock meeting with my IT security people. I want to make sure nobody does to us what somebody has done to Waxman, Gold."

"Okay. Sure." She turned over and stared at the wall as he finished dressing. He bent over and kissed her bare shoulder before leaving. "Thanks. Last night was great. Maybe we can do something like that again sometime."

She was thinking of sometime as a future beyond reach. She waited for the sound of the apartment door closing, then got up to shower herself, a long slow shower in which she tried to concentrate on what her options might be. She needed time, time to think, time to run the numbers and see whether they computed.

When eight o'clock rolled around, she called Penny Stanfield at her personal number. "Hey, Penny, can you do me a big favor? I'm kinda hungover from a big date last night. Any chance I could get you to clock me in? I have no idea when I'll actually make it to the office."

"Sure, I'll clock you in. I'll even boot up your terminal so the log shows you at your desk."

"You're a real pal, Penny. Maybe I can do the same for you sometime."

"Count on it. Now, go make yourself a Virgin Bloody Mary and take a hot bath. Does wonders. Bye."

Toby thought about the bath and the Bloody Mary, but collapsed on the couch instead and went back to sleep.

It was a walk without purpose or destination, as Toby obsessed over her dire dilemma, wondering whether taking her mother's way out might be the best option. When the first plane hit the North Tower at the World Trade Center, she was walking north, away, and so absorbed by her own tragedy, so hyper focused, that the enormity of what was happening did not become more important to her until the South Tower collapsed just before ten. She turned and headed south without understanding why she kept on. When the North Tower collapsed a half hour later, she was close enough that some of the debris reached where she stood.

She was thinking of friends and acquaintances, people she knew, at the same time she couldn't stop herself from mentally computing the economic cost. It took her several seconds to realize that the tragedy, whatever its human and economic cost, had given her a get-out-of-jail-free card. Her accusers were gone, the evidence was gone, everything was gone. She, too, was gone. She would be among the presumed dead whose remains would never be identified. She was among the employees of Waxman, Gold, and Walsh known to be working in their Manhattan offices near the top of the building at 1 World Trade Center, offices destroyed when the building collapsed. Now what?

The flash of the hologram of a driver's license caught her eye as it tumbled down in front of her. She picked it up. It had belonged to a young woman some years her senior, a woman about her height and weight, with a forgettable face. It was an impulsive decision, an instant choice made without Toby's usual analysis or weighing of the alternatives or calculating of the consequences. Louise Bianca Carbone was among the dead, and no one would be looking for her. What if Louise Carbone showed up someplace else, where no one knew her and no one had reason to believe she had died?

If Toby moved fast enough, it might just be possible to pull off a metamorphosis. She was desperate and, for one time in her life, running on purest instinct. She slipped the driver's license into her jacket pocket and started walking back toward her apartment. She was already thinking about where she might go and how she might become Louise Carbone.

Chapter 27

"So, Toby Warner, that's you, huh?" Rand, who had been listening with fists to his cheeks in absorbed attention, finally reached for his tea.

"Yeah, that's me. Or was."

"Well, you did say your story was dark and complicated. And Louise Carbone was also you, all along."

"Always me." She closed her eyes for several seconds. "There was this song I heard at a music festival. My girlfriend and I hitchhiked to the Berkshires in Western Massachusetts. Crazy. We were still in high school, still kids, before I started college. This folk-rock singer—I think his name was Denton Reynolds—did a set. One of his songs was called 'Always Me.' It really hit me in a way that took on new meaning as life went on. I still remember the chorus: 'That was me, this is me, this will be until I'm gone./The verses change, words rearrange, but the chorus is sung on.' That's my anthem. That's me."

"Did you ever look back? Did you ever go back, like, to New York?"

"I drove down for the fifth anniversary observance of the attacks, but I couldn't bring myself to actually enter

Manhattan. I watched from the Jersey side as those eighty-eight spotlights sent their piercing blue beams skyward. They were arranged to represent the footprints of the two towers. 'A Tribute in Light,' it was called. I thought I would cry, but I felt numb, as if I were watching a scene from someone else's life."

"And now it's Shanna Newsom," he said. "Forgive me for having a little trouble getting my head around this. How the hell did it all come about? And what really happened to Louise Carbone?"

"Louise Carbone was created out of thin air, almost literally, in a flash of inspiration and desperation on a Manhattan street corner. Shanna Grace Newsom was the work of years. For a second time, I could see myself needing a new identity, one that would stand up to a certain scrutiny. I needed an actual birth certificate. The real Shanna Grace Newsom, the original, was born a few years before me. I figured with that, I had a chance of looking younger than my supposed age rather than too old. The baby had been premature and never made it out of the hospital, which is how I learned about her, from a death notice, a four-line announcement in the local Cranefield newspaper. I figured the hospital must have messed up the paper work, because I couldn't find a death certificate in Connecticut vital records. That fit my purposes perfectly.

"As I learned just this week, there actually was an official death certificate, but under 'Baby Girl Chandler'; Chandler was the mother's surname on the birth certificate. The baby weighed less than three pounds and lived only five days. I figured I was hurting no one by taking the name, and I have, in a sense, given a tiny lost soul a life story."

"What about the rest of that story?"

"The rest? Well, instead of just making it all up on the fly, I decided to plan it out, chapter by chapter, a novel rather than a work of slam fiction. I would decide what I wanted to be, something that I had some hope of becoming, and then I would make it so.

"All that digging into records and historical documents had taught me a lot. I started becoming connected with the past and realized I actually liked history. I already knew some economics from the three undergrad courses I took at Columbia, and I was always good with numbers. So, I became a quantitative historian specializing in economic history.

"I didn't know where I was headed, but I knew by then I wanted a quiet academic life out of the spotlight. To have that, I needed an advanced degree. At the library, I stumbled on an article about New England private colleges and universities coming under siege and succumbing to demographic change. I had never heard of Kennilwirth, but a doctorate from there would be perfect. I tacked on a master's to add some depth to the story and granted myself a bachelor's from Mount Cherton. Who would ever know? There were no records. no audit trails. To see whether I could pull it off for the long haul, I did some library research and some writing and started submitting papers. Much to my surprise, I was getting published."

"It was that easy?"

"No, it was that hard. This didn't happen overnight, and not just anybody could do what I did. In case you haven't put it together yet, I'm fucking smart."

"And Holcomb? How did all that lead you here?"

"Holcomb University was not even on my radar, because nobody here had published in the little niche I was carving out for myself, but I was on their radar. Somebody here had the bright idea that it might look progressive in the brochures if the university hired faculty specialized in the economic history of African-Americans in the South. I suspect that this particular somebody is long gone."

"And you were doing this while working as a bookkeeper for the mob."

"Not the mob. I cooked books for Joey Forte and Forte Construction; that's not the same. It's more complicated than you think. There are all these connections among the real Mafiosi and the unions and the corrupt state and local officials and the shady businesses up and down the food chain and … It's an entire ecosystem."

"What happened at the end? What happened to the missing money?"

"Well, for one thing, there is no missing money. That's part of the ecosystem I was talking about. The money is with Joey in some off-shore accounts, some of it is with the mob, some in the pockets of corrupt officials, but none of it was ever intended to end up in my pockets. That kind of money is dangerous money. Sooner or later it gets you, whether because the wiseguys catch up with you or the feds find you. Or another rip-off artist rips off the rip-off artists. No, Jess had his fantasies about the big score, which I encouraged, but I had my savings account and that was it.

"Jess and I had different ideas of what would happen next. He thought we'd disappear together after we faked being rubbed out by Joey and his people. I was thinking about a future as Professor Newsom."

"So what went wrong?"

"I still don't know. Jess screwed up somehow, and ended up dead for real. Louise ended up dead for all intents and purposes. Joey got to have his story about being ripped off to the tune of three mil plus, and I got to start over from scratch at Holcomb University."

"And then I came along and changed everything."

"Don't flatter yourself. Don't grant yourself more agency than you deserve."

"You want to know the truth, Shanna? I don't feel like I have any agency, any control. I feel like things are just happening to me, and I'm riding a roller coaster. I just feel lucky that you're in the seat beside me."

"I'm in the car ahead of you. You're watching my back and wishing we were in the same car."

"And you?"

"I'm wishing we were in the same car." She looked at her watch. "And I'm looking at the time and thinking we blew most of the morning. I need to teach two classes and after that we should be thinking about getting ready for dinner with the charming Professor Belknap."

"I'll have to head back to the apartment. I have no idea what to wear."

"Even more importantly, neither of us have any idea what to say. Or ask? We need to talk this through."

"Okay, I'll go shower and change and come back here to take you to dinner at the Deacon's House."

"You're getting ahead of yourself. I'm still your designated driver. After I'm finished teaching, I'll come back here and drive you to your place for you to change. Then I can drive us to the Deacon's House. There's a little parking lot behind there that almost nobody knows."

❧

Shanna was just turning off of Racine Circle when she heard the short pulse of a siren and saw flashing lights behind her. "Oh, shit. What now?"

"It's probably the tail lights," he said. "This model, the tail lights, they can go on and off, at least on this one."

"Just what I need. I start driving again and this sort of thing happens."

"What's this thing with you and driving?"

"I don't have a license."

"I thought you could drive."

"Well, der, what have I been doing all this time as your chauffeur?"

"Driving without a license, I would guess. And now the officer is rapping at your window, and I recognize him from the hospital."

Through the window, the officer's voice was muffled but understandable. "Ma'am, I am asking you one last time to roll down your window. Please show me your license and registration."

Rand ducked down to look up at the officer. "It's my car, officer, registered to me. She's driving me."

"Fine with me, sir, but I still need the registration and her license."

Shanna pursed her lips. "Sooner or later, I knew this would happen. Sooner or later."

"What was that, ma'am?"

"Ah, nothing. I don't have—"

"She doesn't have her license with her. I was in a hurry when we left, and I hassled her to—"

234

"I'm not asking for your life stories, sir. I just need to see her license."

"I don't have it with me, officer," she said, with a sigh.

"Well, then, I am going to have to cite you for driving without a license. You must carry a valid driver's license with you at all times when you are operating a motor vehicle. Do you have some picture identification, ma'am?"

"Yes, here's my faculty keycard. I'm a professor at the University."

He took the card. "Wait a minute here. I remember you." He stooped down to look across at Rand. "And it's you. I'm so sorry, both of you. I didn't know it was you two they was talking about when they told me to wait here and watch for a Civic with the tail lights out."

Rand pointed at the officer. "Are you saying you were sent here to look for us?"

"Well, not you exactly, just a Honda Civic. Again, I am sorry. I think what you did was pretty amazing, Mr. McMurphy. That could've been my son running across the parking lot."

Rand leaned across in front of Shanna and held out his hand toward the patrolman. "I'm a father too, Julio. I lost my son, so I know what it's all about."

They clasped hands and nodded in perfect synch. "Stay cool, bro," the policeman said. "Stay cool," the ex-cop said.

Julio left, the floodlights on the patrol car winked out, and the car swung out and sped off into the fading light.

Shanna sat for a moment. "What just happened? Male bonding trumps the law?"

Rand gave her a big smile. "I never realized before just this minute how hard it must be for you, for women. All I know is how hard it is for me, for us men, to make sense of what is going on with you, between women, any two women on the planet. It must be something like that for you, I suppose. I mean, that was just me and Julio—I don't even remember his last name, but he was the cop at Mercy Hospital—and for a moment we were just two men, two fathers, thinking about our sons, reaching across a gulf of race and experience too wide to be measured. I'm white and he's—what is it okay to say these days?—brown, and right then we're just dad's. Can you understand that?"

"No, and not because I'm a woman. I know about that sense of sisterhood. No, it's not that. But I've never been a mother, and that makes a difference. It all makes a difference. There are limits to understanding. I've never had a child, but you have. Darlene has. Neither of us is Black, but she is. You're male and she and I aren't." Shanna's face lit up. "God, it's so simple and obvious, trite even, and yet so fundamental. We are all of us stuck in settling, in a universe of good enough. We satisfice because there is no other way."

"And I reject that, Shanna. There are limits to everything, but that doesn't mean we need to—or should—limit ourselves, our reach, our aspirations. I want it all, whether I can have it or not. With you, I want it all."

Shanna was gripping the steering wheel so tightly that her knuckles were blanched. "Me too. With you I want it all, everything."

"I hope you realize what you are asking for, because everything is a fucking long shopping list.'

"I know. Let's get you dressed and us ready for dinner. We need to start working on that list."

Chapter 28

Professor Belknap greeted them at the door with arms spread in welcome. "Do come in. And thank you for being fashionably late, giving us time to accommodate a last-minute addition to the guest list."

Shanna scrunched up her face. "I'm sorry about that, but I realized today that I could hardly leave our wounded Professor McMurphy to ache alone at home while I was out partying with you. I hope it hasn't put you to too much trouble."

"Not too much. Tereza usually makes more than enough of everything in any event, which is a continual challenge to my waistline, and it only takes a minute to set an extra place at the table. So, welcome, both of you. We can start with drinks on the veranda. I want to hear all about your heroics, Randall."

"Hardly anything heroic. And please, my friends call me Rand."

"Well then, Rand, it's an honor to have you in my home—while it is still my home."

"So, you are finally retiring?" Shanna said. "I remember

when I first arrived and you took me under your wing, you declared you would never retire, ever, that they would have to carry you bodily from the classroom."

"Did I say that? What did I know? I was still young, in my sixties. But, yes, I am retiring. And I finally realized it was pointless of me to come back in the fall just to teach one course and to complete the calendar year. So, in a matter of weeks, I say goodbye to classes and syllabus revisions and all that rigmarole that makes up the academic life."

"What will you do with yourself?" Rand asked.

"Slow my steps to a walking pace, draw on a lifetime of reading and research to start writing some really good stories, and generally enjoy the good life in a villa by the sea."

"Shanna tells me you might be headed for Tuscany."

"Well, not right away. I have some research to wrap up and students to supervise through their own research. So I'll be down in the islands for a while. In fact, I fly over to Bermuda next week to finish arrangements for the summer research. But enough talk about academic oldsters. I want to hear about young heroes, so let's get our drinks and enjoy the evening air."

On the veranda, Shanna stood aside as the men talked. She watched Rand going over the events in Taggertsville, which had, in a week of interviews and encounters, become a rehearsed recollection with well-paced pauses and added color and detail. She was thinking about the way people edit their own stories, how, over time, the story becomes the reality and the ground truth fades. What she had been doing in her historical work was reaching back to recover ground truth, using hard data to build new stories that could replace the redacted and much revised old ones. What she had been doing in her life had been almost the opposite, turning story into reality. She shivered.

Rand had noticed. "Are you quite all right, Shanna?"

"I'm fine, just a chill breeze."

"Well then," Gareth said, "before the evening breezes chill us too much, let us repair to the dining room. I'll let Tereza know we're ready."

~

Dinner featured chicken paprikash—"a specialty of Tereza and a favorite of mine," Gareth said—and a decanter of a well-chilled rosé that kept being refilled when no one was looking.

"Strange," Gareth said, toward the end of dinner, "that whole business with the old tunnel and the discovery of the body. It puzzles me still."

Rand raised his eyebrows. "In what way?"

"Why would students—if it was students as is claimed—why would they be making a hole in the wall at the back of a storage closet in the first place? It hardly seems the sort of thing that is done on a dare or a lark. It seemed, the whole thing, to be such a deliberated endeavor. Very puzzling."

"And do you have a theory, Professor?" he prodded.

"Gareth, please. If I can call you Rand, you can call me Gareth. And, no, I don't have an hypothesis. That sort of speculation would seem to be more in your domain, detective work, that is."

"Not anymore. I retired from detective work; now I teach."

"Retired? I heard you were some kind of super sleuth who sweeps in and solves old mysteries. Cold cases, I believe they are called in the argot of your field."

"Uh, yes, that's right. But how did you know?"

"I'm an anthropologist, Rand, anthropologists learn things by paying attention. We observe and understand cultures, like the culture of academia and the culture of Holbrook University faculty. Word gets around in this culture; very little goes unnoticed, especially by the trained observer."

"I'm rather at a disadvantage here," Gareth said, "because I'm a newcomer to this culture, still very much an outsider. You, on the other hand, are senior faculty here, on the cusp of becoming emeritus, as they say in the argot of the culture. You must know the culture, the history, inside out."

Shanna, the bystander, watched in fascination as the two men bobbed and weaved in their verbal joust.

"Insider? Outsider?" Gareth said. "In anthropology, neither view is considered privileged. Each has its own reality with its own argument for validity. The goal of the ethnography, which is what I do, is to go inside, to immerse completely within a culture, to experience it as a participant, but at the same time to remain apart as the observer, to become a participant observer, as we say."

"Sounds tricky, maybe impossible. You can't be in two places at once."

"Tricky yes, but impossible? Well, I certainly hope not, or my entire academic career adds up to naught. And, no, perhaps you can't be in two places at once, but you can, with practice and effort, hold two irreconcilable views in mind at the same time."

"I have this feeling," Rand said, "that something like that is happening in our conversation right now, that it appears to be about one thing while it is actually about something altogether different."

"Or it is actually about one thing and simultaneously about the other. We can be talking about the conceptual underpinnings of a discipline and also talking about recent events on this campus. Both-and. Things can be one thing and its opposite at the same time."

"But, professor ... Gareth, this sounds more like word-games and riddles than like reality. What do you think really happened with that whole tunnel discovery?"

"That is what I was asking you?"

Rand looked to Shanna, his expression one of pleading for help. She set down her fork and turned to Gareth. "If it was not students on some secret but silly mission, who might it be? Just for the sake of argument." Did he know? she wondered. What did he know? And what would he be prepared to admit to?

"Well, Shanna, for the sake of argument, it might be someone who digs into things, someone who digs things up. That someone could be like any of those who formed our short-lived local investigatory group. Let's see, who did we have?" He started ticking off on his fingers. "We had an historian, an archeologist, a criminologist, and, oh yes, an anthropologist, all disciplines eminently qualified, and with good reason, for unraveling riddles of the past."

"Are you suggesting it was one of us, one of that group, who broke into the library and the old tunnel?"

"Hardly that, Shanna. We were talking about theory; I was posing a conceptual line of inquiry, merely for the sake of argument." He leaned toward Rand. "And that, for the benefit of the relative newcomer in our midst, is how it goes in the culture of Academe. 'For the sake of argument' could well be a motto tattooed on our foreheads. It is what we do. 'For the sake of argument' is part of the culture, the cultural lifeblood." He retrieved his napkin from his lap and carefully refolded it. "And now, with all that settled, would you two please join me in the library for an after-dinner sip of something. I have an excellent Armagnac that I could recommend. Or whatever."

తా

At the door, as the three of them were saying their goodnights, Gareth gave Shanna a hug. "We have, you and I, more in common than meets the eye," he whispered. "Thank you for that."

On the short drive back to Racine Circle, Rand kept shaking his head. "What was that all about? It made no sense. The whole evening made no sense."

"It made perfect sense. He spelled it all out."

"Then enlighten me, please."

"He knows we were the perpetrators, he knows we're investigating him and his past, and he's telling us things may not be what they seem. He's also warning us off, reminding us not to ask questions if we're not ready for the answers."

"And how do you get all that?"

"From the subtext, from the way he deflected direct questions over the entire evening."

"I thought he was just being evasive."

"It was evasion, but it was also protection. Both-and, as he said."

"He was protecting himself."

"Yes, and he was protecting us."

"How do you get that?"

"Both-and."

⇜

On a calm May afternoon, three weeks shy of the end of his last semester teaching, Gareth took off in his pontoon-equipped customized Cessna 172 from a site on the barrier islands. His filed flight plan took him to the south and east, skirting a weather front building up at sea, and arriving at the Bermuda coast shortly before sunset.

Gareth had been flying small planes for most of his adult life, but float-planes were a new thing for him. Two years earlier, he had decided to pursue getting his FAA Single Engine Sea Rating to give him greater freedom in island hopping, and the previous year he had his Cessna refitted with pontoons.

The conditions en route to Bermuda were just acceptable, but he had committed to meetings the following day. Between the expansion fuel tank installed in the cargo area and the fact that he was flying without passengers and almost no baggage, he had more than enough safety margin for the six-and-a-half-hour flight at the Cessna's droning pace.

Some three hours out, with the headwinds picking up and the seas below roughening, Gareth admitted defeat and called air traffic control to announce he was turning back and heading home. Ten minutes later, the Cessna disappeared from radar. By nightfall, it had still not arrived at the harbor on the coast. Air and sea searches began the next day, but turned up nothing until the following day, when a few pieces of debris were spotted some twenty nautical miles south of Belknap's last known location. A ship recovered the debris, which were confirmed to be from a white Cessna.

Commencement exercises at the end of the month included a moment of silence for a professor whom the Chancellor called "an icon of the university, and a beacon of inspiration for generations of students."

Part 5 – Abigail:

Chapter 29

Aided by his cane,

Rand stubbornly made his way down the path from Stergeson Hall and the athletic field to the house on Racine Circle. He could have gone by way of the road, but he was determined to take the shorter footpath. When he let himself in with his new key, Shanna was already home. "You're early," he said.

"You're late. I think you've been shirking your training regimen," she teased, "not keeping up the jogging pace like you used to."

"I'll have to get back into training, then. Do you know a coach who could help a wounded ex-cop, maybe somebody with rehab experience?" He put on a pleading puppy-dog face.

"No, but I know a first-class massage therapist who might help you feel better." She spread her arms in an I'm-here gesture.

"I'll take it. And how was your day?"

"Good. I got the new research approved."

"Oh, what's that?"

"Historical research: I am still an historian, you know. Anyway, we have access to the Deacon's House for one week, in cooperation with the University archivist and the official university historian. The university is planning to do another round of renovations over the summer and open it up for tours in the fall. There's also a faction that wants to turn it into a bed-and-breakfast. You know, spend the night in a piece of Southern history. I just want to poke around and see what I can learn."

"You're not giving up, are you? The man's dead, case closed."

"That's not how I understood it works. With homicide, or suspected homicide, a case is always fair game. Besides, you're the cold-case expert. I'm just an historian pursuing her research."

"He died in a plane crash."

"I'm not talking about the professor; I'm talking about the professor's wife."

"You're still on the Abigail case?"

"Still on it, and with the professor gone, more intrigued than ever. Want to do some more digging? You're not the only one with new keys." She held up a Holcomb University keyring carrying several conventional brass keys.

"Don't we have to do this with the university people?"

"Technically, yes, but nobody told me I couldn't go in on my own, and I didn't ask. Want to join me?"

"Now?"

"No, after dinner."

"What's for dinner?"

"The usual Thursday-night special, microwave pizza."

"With the usual house wine, I suppose. What is it this week, Bordeaux-by-the-Box? Maybe I should have accepted Darlene's offer to stay at her place while I was recuperating.

Certainly the food would be better."

"It's not too late. You want to go back to your darling Darlene? The car keys are in the basket by the door."

Rand was a little taken aback by the edge in her voice. "I was just teasing."

"And I was just telling you there are no shackles on you."

"You want me to leave? You just have to say it, and I'll get out of your hair. I know where the car keys are kept. Besides, it's my car. And it still makes me nervous that you drive without a license."

"Well, if it makes you so nervous, then you drive. I'm sure a bullet wound wouldn't stop you from playing the macho man, stoically making the painful sacrifice."

Rand took a step back. "What is happening here? One minute we're teasing, and the next minute it morphs into a fight. And this keeps happening. Maybe I should go back to my place, give you some space."

"And give you a chance to play the martyr, struggling up and down three flights of stairs."

"Two. It's only on the third floor. It's basic math: floor three minus floor one equals two."

"That does it!" She threw the keys for the Deacon's House at him but her aim was high. His left hand shot up and caught them. "What is happening to us?" he said.

She plunked down on the sofa, her whole body slumped in defeat. "It's not working."

"What's not working?"

"Us. This."

"Maybe. But maybe this is just how it goes."

"And you're the one who said you want it all, that you were done with satisfying. What are we going to do?"

He started to sit down beside her. "Scrunch over and make room."

"There, that's it, that's at least part of the problem. This is a small house and your apartment is even smaller."

"And both of us have been living alone for a lot of years, add that into the mix. We've gotten used to having space and to doing things however we want whenever we want without having to take anyone else into account."

"You're right," she said, "and I hate it when you're so right."

"Yeah, because you want to be the one that's right."

"And there you go again, being so right. We're doomed, Rand, we're doomed. I don't know whether to laugh or cry."

"Both. I think we have a lot to learn, but I don't think we're doomed. Look, we both have had to reinvent ourselves. Who says we can't do that for the two of us together. We figure out who we want to be as a couple and make it so, turn the story into reality. You, of all people, know something about how to pull that off."

She put her head on his shoulder. "Okay, yes. I want to try. I love you, and I want to try."

"And I love you, and I want to try. There, we both said the L word, right out loud. That's a start.

"I'm scared."

"Me too, but we do things one step at a time." He stood up. "Starting with this whole food business. I already know you like good food, but you settle for such slop in your own home."

"I can't cook. No, wait, I probably can—or could, if I wanted to—but I really never liked cooking. It's a nuisance, just something that has to be done and gotten out of the way in order to have something on the table."

"Then why do it?"

"I can't afford to eat out or eat takeout all the time."

"But you have other options. Who says you have to cook? Look around, you're not the only one here."

"You cook?"

"Hell yes. I may not have studied at the Culinary Institute of America, but I've picked up a lot in my years of living alone, and Darlene is always passing on pointers. Look, you go do something in your little office and close the door behind you. I'll let you know when dinner is ready."

"But I hardly have anything in the house and—"

"Go, do some work, and don't be such a control freak. Let me see what I can do with what you have."

Forty minutes later he tapped on the closed door to her home office. "Dinner's ready whenever you are."

She stepped out and her face lit up. "Wow, candles. And the paper napkins folded so nicely. What's the occasion?"

"The first day of our new story, the one we're making up about us."

"And the pizza? That doesn't look like the one I bought."

"Well, I did some things with it, pan-roasted some frozen veggies, chopped up the last bit of salami to sprinkle on top. And pizza comes out so much better from the toaster oven than the microwave."

"And what's this in our glasses?"

"Try it."

She took a sip. "Mmm, that's good. Sangria?"

"An inferior box wine plus a little orange juice and cinnamon sugar and you have a pretty good sangria."

"I could never do this. I just don't think like you."

"And I don't think like you, but that doesn't mean you couldn't do this. But, as I said before, why cook if you don't like to? Let me do that. As long as we're living together, even if it is temporary, let's write our own work roster. It's our storyline, and we can always edit it as needed. So, sit down, enjoy my pastiche pizza and ersatz sangria, and after dinner let me follow your lead on your clandestine historical research."

The solar-powered path lights in front were the only lights on at the Deacon's House. Rand held a flashlight as Shanna unlocked the front door and felt around for the light switch. The porch light came on. She switched it off and tried another. Across the room, an antique floor lamp with a tasseled shade lit the room with a warm soft light.

"Let's start with the library," she said, "then I want to check out the annex where the professor lived."

In the library she slipped a green clothbound book from the shelf. "Look at this. It's a limited edition private printing from a small press up in Durham. 'A Van Der Houten Odyssey.' I tried to get a copy for my research, but couldn't track one down. And all along there was a copy right here on campus in Gareth Belknap's private library." She started flipping through pages. "I knew the family was Dutch, but I had forgotten that they came by way of Aruba and Curaçao in what was then the Dutch West Indies. I wonder if that is what started Gareth's interest in the islands, the fact that his wife's family had roots in the Caribbean."

Across the room, Rand was entranced by the shelf on plants, and had already laid out several books on the reading table. "Make sure you put those back in the right places," she told him. "The professor was very meticulous about keeping things in alphabetical order within the Dewey Decimal Classification."

"Did you ever take a look at this stuff?" he said. "It's very interesting."

"Yeah, medical anthropology was his thing: tropical plants, folk medicine, spiritual healing, all that stuff."

"Yeah, yeah, but I'm looking at these forensically."

"How so?"

"Books record more than their contents; they record their use. You just have to let them speak for themselves."

"What do you mean?"

"Well, corners get turned, margins become annotated, pages become smudged by dirty fingers. Just by scanning a shelf, you can see which books have had the most use, sometimes which was most recently read or referenced. One of the simplest things you can do is let the book open itself, letting gravity gently spread its pages. Take a look at these four books, all among the more heavily used from that particular shelf, and look at the pages where they naturally opened themselves to."

Shanna walked over to the reading table and looked at the opened books one-by-one. "I don't see it. They're all different, published at different times, about different kinds of plants. What's the pattern? What are you seeing?"

"What a homicide detective might notice more than an historian. Look again."

She scanned the open pages again. "Oh, wow! They're all poisons, poisonous plants."

"Bingo, and in several other books, if you fan through

them, the dirtiest pages are also mostly about poisons. Even for a medical anthropologist, Professor Belknap had an unusual fascination with poisons."

"Well, maybe that makes legitimate sense. Many medicines have been derived from or based on plant poisons. Digitalis or curare, for example."

"True, but I still see a consistent pattern."

They continued to work their way around the room, noting titles of books with signs of heavy use, sometimes slipping them out and scanning the interiors.

"And over here we have the chart books, travel guides, and the map collection," Rand said. "No surprises here. Caribbean, Caribbean, and more Caribbean."

"The surprise is in what is not there," she said.

"There's a lot that isn't there. What are you seeing? Or not seeing?"

"Italy, Tuscany. Wouldn't you expect that a man who talked so much about wanting to retire there would have done some reading about it?"

"Well, he could have done that through the library, borrowed books."

"Look around you, Rand. The man was a collector. Many of these books actually belong to the university library, but he kept them out on permanent loan. No, this is another pattern to note and place in the 'meaning not yet known' file. Enough book research for the moment. Let's move on to the annex."

The annex comprised a bedroom with en suite bath on one side of a short hallway, and a study and storage room on the other side. The roomy study held an antique roll-top desk with a modern office posture chair, a utility table spread with navigation charts, and a tall bookcase topped by a scale model of a pontoon-equipped Cessna 172. On the walls were framed snapshots of the professor with various student research teams from over the years. Three side chairs, apparently for meetings with students, were arranged in a semi-circle facing the desk and posture chair.

"This feels weird," she said. "It's different doing this sort of digging when the owner just died. Not the same as looking at the belongings of someone who died a century ago."

"Weird to you, not to me. Let's check out the desk." He slid up the roll-top. A computer mouse and mouse pad suggested that the professor had worked with a laptop at the desk. To the left was a small framed color photo of a smiling young woman with a round face and curly blond hair. "That's Abigail," Shanna said. "I've seen a few other pictures of her. She was pretty. And so young. Barely out of her teens when she died."

The interior of the desk was partitioned into the traditional cubbyholes and small shelves of antique desks. "He was a collector, all right" Rand said. "Here we have his old passports and just below that his old pilot logbooks. Good place to start. You take the passports, and I'll check the flight logs to see what we can learn."

They each took a stack, sat down in adjacent side chairs, and started paging through years of Professor Belknap's life. Ten minutes later, Shanna closed the last of the canceled passports.

"Well, what did you find?" Rand said.

"I didn't find the same thing I didn't find in the library. Gareth has never been to Italy. He's been to Brazil, Indonesia, England, lots of places, probably conferences, judging from the timing and short stays, and he's made a number of what were likely holiday trips to the Netherlands, and, of course, countless trips all around the Caribbean. But Italy? Never."

"Okay, so maybe it was his dream, a fantasy, or a place-holder for an undecided destination."

"Or maybe he never intended to end up in Italy."

"All right, all right," he said. "Let's see what else we can learn here."

The books shelved in the office were mostly textbooks and general reference books, including bilingual dictionaries for Spanish, French, Portuguese, and Dutch. "I know," he said. "You don't have to say it. No Italian. Let's check out the charts and maps on the table."

"I already did when we first came in. They're from his field work last summer."

"How do you know?"

"Because last summer was the first year he was flying his float plane. He told me all about how he had to fit an extra gas tank to his plane and could only take two students because the pontoons made the plane less efficient, so the range was more limited. He was very excited about the trip and how he was going to island hop because of the shorter range, but also to get more experience in water landings and takeoffs. He showed me the maps—those maps—and traced the route, all the way to St. Thomas, in the U.S. Virgin Islands, where he was collaborating with some professor at the university there. He was like a kid with a new toy. He loved flying. That's a model of Charlotte, his plane, over there on the bookcase."

"Huh, why Charlotte. His wife's name was Abigail."

"The state capitol? I don't know."

"Okay, those were last year's maps. Supposedly he had the ones for this year with him. Good. Let's move on to the bedroom."

The bedroom was as neat as the rest of the house, not surprising given that the fastidious professor also had a housekeeper. On the nightstand was another picture of Abigail and in front of it, a leather-bound diary. "I used to keep a diary," Shanna said, picking it up.

"You don't anymore?"

"No, too dangerous. Diaries carry personal secrets, and diaries can be read by others. What remains in your head stays yours. Funny, I wouldn't think of Gareth as the type to keep a diary." She opened it up. "Wow, this is Abigail's diary." She fanned through the pages. "No wonder it's mostly blank." She sat down on the edge of the bed and started reading.

"While you dig into Abigail's secrets, I'll look around and check out the storage room."

Fifteen minutes later when he returned, he found Shanna with the open diary face down in her lap and tears in her eyes. "What? What did you learn?" he said.

Shanna wiped her eyes. "I learned that she was so in love and so deeply unhappy."

"Really? That's not what everybody else said. I heard they were a happy couple."

"They were in love, yes, and Abigail knew how much Gareth loved her and wanted her to be happy. So, for him she was happy—for a time. It became something she did— the happy face, the happy smile, the happy laugh— for him and the rest of the world. But he was an anthropologist, and he could see what was really going on, and it broke his heart. At one point in her diary she writes 'I would rather die in a bright villa, than live in a dark museum.' Later she writes of desperately wanting a way out, any way out, about the pain of dying being preferable to the pain of love. There are pages of poetry written out of her isolation. Here's one she titled 'Birdstrike'."

> A nameless bird flies
> into a clouded sky
> painted by reflected lies
> in glass, a crystal void already filled.
> Stunned, she falls, is stilled,
> then rises, shaken,
> to chase a different light.
> I wander an unfenced landscape,
> prison grounds without escape,
> and walk toward a wood that promises a path,
> but deadfalls block the way.
> I turn, mistaken,
> to chase a different dark.

"There are pages where tears have made the ink run, although I don't know whether they were her tears or Gareth's. Obviously, he's read the diary; it was here by his bed. How much that must have hurt when he learned of her sadness and her desperation."

"Do you think he killed her? Or maybe he helped her commit suicide?"

"No, I think the story is something different, especially after I read the last entry in her diary. Here, read it."

He took the diary from her. "Okay. She writes, 'I have

been reading the diary of that Dutch girl, the one hiding in the attic, and I have come to believe there is hope, that even in an imprisoned life, a life of isolation, one might find some happiness, some way to look to a tomorrow in which love continues, a tomorrow of love.' Wow."

"Yeah, now we know."

"What? What do we know?"

"Look at that last entry again, carefully, the whole thing."

He squinted and scanned the page, puzzlement painting his face.

"Read it as if you were an historian," she prompted him.

His mouth opened and his face lit up. "Oh my God!"

"Yes. Oh my God. And we have some field research to organize."

Chapter 30

The non-stop flight

from Charlotte, North Carolina, landed at Cyril King Airport just before two o'clock on a sunny afternoon under clear skies with temperatures in the high eighties and a steady breeze out of the east. Shanna and Rand collected their bags and stepped out onto the island of St. Thomas.

"We'll stay overnight in town, in Charlotte Amalie," she said, "then begin our field research tomorrow."

"And I know what we can do tonight," he said. "Darlene suggested a place for fabulous fish tacos based on recommendations from her fellow chefs and foodie friends."

"Sounds good. I'm excited. I've never been out of the country before."

"You're not out of the country, remember. This is the U.S. Virgin Islands."

"Yeah, I know, but it feels like it in some ways. Don't you think?"

"I wouldn't know. I've never been out of the country before, either. What boring lives we've led, wouldn't you say?" They both laughed.

⁓

In the shortening shadows of late morning, they took a taxi out of Charlotte Amalie and then got out to walk the rest of the way. In the rising heat, they hiked slowly along the road up the point, past gated estates and grand houses. "Nice neighborhood," Rand said. "Are you sure about this? Will we know what we're looking for when we see it?"

"Yes, and there it is." She pointed to a large two-story pink and blue stucco house set well back from the road.

"Are you sure?"

"Look at the sign." In recessed letters on the wall by the driveway were the words, "Villa Toscana."

"How did you know that?"

"Google maps."

They walked up the drive and rang the bell beside the massive carved front door. A pretty woman with curly ash-blond hair answered the door. "Yes, can I help you? If you're looking for the Werkmann place, you just passed it."

"Abigail?"

The woman smiled and frowned at the same time. "Do I know you?"

"Abigail van der Houten?"

"I ... I think you must ..."

"We have something that belongs to you." Shanna held out the diary.

The woman's face blanched. "I don't know what ..."

"It's all right, Abby, they're friends of mine." Gareth Belknap's raspy baritone voice was unmistakable as he entered from the other room. "These are the people I was telling you about. Please, Shanna and Rand, come in. Welcome to Villa Toscana. I see you found the diary."

"Hidden in plain sight. Yes, we found it."

"Excellent. Would you care to join Abby and me for some punch overlooking the water? You and Abby should get to know each other. I think we all have a great deal to talk about, a great deal indeed."

The back of the house looked out over a sand beach on a sheltered cove. Gareth moved chairs around on the tiled veranda as Abigail brought out a tray of tall glasses filled with ice and a green-gold concoction.

"I hope you like this," Gareth said. "It's one of Tereza's specialties. I have no idea what she puts in it, but it's icy ambrosia."

"Tereza? That Tereza? Your cook is here?"

"Well, she needed a job after the university let her go without notice, so, now she's here, still cooking for me."

Rand accepted one of the glasses and walked over to look down toward the beach. "I suppose that's your float plane down there at the dock."

"Yes, that's Charlotte. I'm afraid she's a bit worse for wear after the flight down. I ended up having to set down in open ocean in order to refill the auxiliary fuel tank. I thought I could do it while flying, but that proved to require ambidextrous coordination beyond my abilities. So I circled and picked a relatively smooth patch, then did a very unpretty water landing. I refilled the auxiliary—made a mess of it—then dumped the fuel canisters and some bogus debris. The whole thing was a bit dicey, and I wasn't certain I was going to get airborne again, but ... here I am."

"But you disappeared from radar?"

"I disappeared when I landed, and it's a small plane and waves can do funny things with radar. After I finally took off again, I was flying as low as I dared, mostly in the dark. I figured even if I was spotted, no self-respecting air traffic controller would believe what they were seeing. I do think I was spotted by at least one ship, but, there again, they probably wrote it off as a glitch."

"So you risked dying to fake your own death."

"I risked dying to live out the rest of my life fulltime with Abby." He put his arm around Abby's waist and she looked up at him.

"Not his first attempt at faking a death, either," she said.

Gareth looked over at Shanna. "Indeed, and I'm not the only one here with experience in that black art."

Abby looked uncertain as to whether to speak. "Are there still more things you haven't told me?"

"Only the ones I haven't gotten around to yet, dear. As we both know, keeping secrets between anthropologists is all but impossible."

"You're an anthropologist too?" Shanna asked her.

"Yes, urban ethnography. Gareth inspired me, got me interested. It took me a long time to get my degree, but I finally did. We've collaborated on more than a few projects."

"I don't remember your name on any of his papers."

"We publish independent papers and play games with the acknowledgments. He might express his thanks to Amalie Avilla or I will credit help from Gerhardt Bell-Knopf. It's word games. Neither one of us was out to build the biggest corpus. We were having fun."

"But you lived apart."

"Yes, we had one of the very first of those long-distance marriages, very long distance, but we spent an awful lot of time together, what between conferences and holidays and joint research, and just many interspersed visits. Plenty of time, but never so much that we tired of each other or felt crowded. Besides, we have more than enough space in our villa." She spread her arms. "Do you like it?"

"It's beautiful, very impressive."

"You must let me give you the complete tour later, but right now I want to pick up a dropped thread of conversation. Gareth said something about faking death, and I saw something flash across your face, Shanna."

"You did?"

"She did," Gareth said. "And so did I. We are both keen observers, not just because we are both anthropologists, but also because people who reinvent themselves have to pay close attention to the people around them."

Shanna could feel her heartbeat speeding up as she looked at Gareth. "You know?"

"I knew from the very beginning that you were making it up, that you had never been part of the grad school scene. You had the data and the credentials, but no sense of the culture. Once I knew where you graduated from—allegedly graduated—I concluded that if I started tracing out your past, I would reach a point where the past vanished. I knew that you had once been someone else. I left it at that, out of respect for you, but also in acknowledgment of my own fictions. In the end, I trusted you, whoever you were. It's a gut thing. Not everything needs rational explanation. And here you are."

"How did you find us?" Abby asked.

"We followed the trail Gareth left. The diary was the last piece of the puzzle. It had so obviously been left out for us to find, and then, well ..."

"And then you read my story. Don't be embarrassed, I'm not. When you two started pursuing the story and getting closer and closer, Gareth and I talked a lot about what to do. He convinced me to trust that our story would be safe with you because your story would be safe with us." Abby smiled warmly. "An unwritten pact of mutual discretion, he called it."

"That's what I figured," Shanna said, "as soon as I saw the last entry in your diary, the one dated two days after your disappearance. I knew we were being entrusted with a secret. But I don't yet know your whole story."

"Nor do I know yours, but we'll talk. Please, say you'll at least have lunch with us or, better, spend the afternoon and stay for dinner."

☙

Over lunch, Shanna found herself telling her story for the second time in less than a month. Once again, she allowed herself to remember being Toby and Louise and becoming Shanna.

"How remarkable," Abigail said. "What you did academically is very similar to what I did, only I had it easier because I never aspired to the academic life. In fact I was running from that world. I didn't need to build up my CV to get hired or apply for grants. I was just having fun on my own. For my publications, I used my initials and my mother's maiden name without any affiliation. A. K. Visscher. Going by just your initials can be an advantage for a woman trying to get published in a man's game, as I'm sure you know."

"I understand. But how did you fund your work? Even plane tickets cost money, and then there's equipment and publication fees and … Do forgive me, but I'm an economic historian and a numbers fanatic, and the numbers in your and Gareth's case don't add up."

"Well, I can start the story, but Gareth will have to finish it." She paused to take a sip of water. "I was only a girl when I fell in love with this tall and handsome older man who spoke of worlds I had only dreamed of and played with ideas that shot off still more ideas like a sparkler in a July night. It should never have been allowed to happen, but it did, and I have no regrets." She took another sip.

"I grew up in wealth, the spoiled but abused—yes, I can say that—only child of a bully. My father never struck me, mind you, but his words could sting far worse than any whip. Until Gareth came along, I was—and here I must be brutally honest—waiting for my father to die so I could inherit the estate and do as I please.

"Where my father belittled me, Gareth elevated me; where my father ignored me, Gareth doted on me. You can see the dynamics being played out, clichéd as they are. Gareth promised me everything, new versions of the luxury in which I had grown up, only with love and affection and freedom. He promised me the world. Except, he had no money and never would. I stood to inherit from my father, but he showed no sign of dying anytime soon. He had set up a trust fund for me, but it would not become mine until I turned twenty-five, which, at eighteen, seemed like a lifetime away.

"Married life was a mix of misery and joy. We were in love and, when we were on our own, brought each other great pleasure, but I was also just a teenager awkwardly thrust into the peculiar culture of university faculty, a culture that looked on me not as a faculty wife but as a student in the wrong place. Even worse, they regarded Gareth as a predatory old man and an all-around embarrassment.

"I had gone from having the run of an enormous house with servants and visiting friends and relatives to being mistress of a cramped cottage on Racine Circle, where I spent my days alone, waiting for Gareth's return. I wanted my father's money so we could buy our way into something better. With time on my hands, I cooked up this outrageous scheme of bidding for my father's sympathies and appealing to some well-hidden latent generosity so he would release the trust fund to me early."

"But then you became ill, right?"

"I didn't become ill, I made myself ill. Or rather Gareth did. It took every wile I could wield to get him to play along with my plan, but he devised a concoction from tropical plant extracts that would make it seem like I was dying."

"Poisons!"

"Yes, basically. My father was supposed to visit me on my deathbed, offer to do anything to save me, and release the trust fund, maybe even throw in a new house or two. Instead, he grew furious and told Gareth I would get nothing and he would get nothing. He was a bully to the end, which came sooner than expected. The official story was that he died of a heart attack, but, as I was to learn many years later, there might have been more to the story.

"Shortly afterwards, we moved into the Deacon's House, which was supposed to be a step up for us, a big old house, but it was a living museum in which only a small part was really ours. I went from misery to greater misery. I was dying in that house. I wanted to get out, but I didn't want to lose Gareth.

"There had been one abduction and murder on campus the previous year, and we decided to use that as a model for our own melodrama. I staged the whole thing while Gareth was away at a conference so he would have an airtight alibi. I traveled by train and bus all the way to Florida. In flower-patched jeans and carrying a backpack, I was anonymous, inconspicuous, just another young student on holidays. I used the last of my cash to stay in a hotel waiting for Gareth to come down for the start of his research and to fly us to St. Thomas, which meant we didn't need passports and never had to clear customs. I've lived here ever since."

"But how did you get this place?" Shanna asked. "I thought you were poor as church mice at that time."

Gareth leaned forward. "I can tell this part. Initially, we were renting. We didn't buy this place until the life insurance payout, and even then, we took out a big mortgage because we wanted to invest most of the insurance money and build it up."

"But where did the rent money come from?" Shanna asked. "How did you manage for the seven years until you got the insurance payout?"

"Well, I had just been promoted to full professor and made dean of the department, for one thing. For another, I had free housing and a discretionary research budget from the university. At that time, living on the island was much less expensive than it is today. When you add it all up, we were fairly well off."

"Hold on there. In rapid succession, you essentially get a house given to you, you get promoted, and you get a research stipend to spend as you choose. How? Why?"

"So, Shanna, did you ever track down what happened to

the van der Houten wealth?"

"Yes, I did. It went to his alma mater, Holcomb University."

"And he dies not long after he changes his will. Suspicious?"

"Let me guess, you know what happened. The university was somehow connected with his death. But how?"

"I don't actually know. I never found out, but at the time, I could see the pattern as clear as 'mene tekel' written on the wall. I approached the then Chancellor as if I were concerned that somebody may have done something that could reflect badly on the university, that maybe an investigation ought to be launched. I also took the occasion to lament my personal straits and slow professional progress on the faculty. The Chancellor asked me to sit on the information for a few days while he looked into things. When he came back to me, he said he had looked into matters and concluded there was nothing needing investigation. He also said the university had created this new fund for faculty support and offered me the house and the stipend. Off the record, he said I was being considered for department chair, which would include promotion to full professor.

"In effect, by bribing me, he admitted the university was somehow implicated in Marcus van der Houten's death."

"Wow, another unsolved murder."

"Probably not a murder, more likely undue influence. Not long before the old man died, he had been subject to aggressive appeals from the university. I think they feared that, if Abigail were to challenge the will, their pressure might come out and they could lose the money. They were bribing both of us, and it really didn't cost them all that much. Besides, our lawyer looked into the changed will and said we had essentially no chance of prevailing if we challenged it."

☙

The rest of the afternoon was taken up by a long walk around the cove, followed by a grand tour of Villa Toscana. At the end of the tour, Rand posed a question to Gareth. "Abigail said that she had no regrets. What about you? Any regrets?"

"Every living person has regrets, but mine are mostly small. Mostly."

"And the ones that are not small?"

"We never had children. That would probably make the list, although it would have been impossible. Once we committed to the peripatetic life of being in more than one place at a time, it was out of the question. But, in another life ..."

Abigail squeezed his hand. "That's a favorite expression of his, right behind 'for the sake of argument' and 'consider the alternative'. Gareth and I have lived double lives, a two-for-one deal. Even now, the neighbors know us as Abigail and Gareth Houten, I suppose because I've been here so much more. At least until now.

"Maybe what we did was wrong, maybe it was a mistake, but I don't think it was a mistake to try. We've done a lot of good work, we've had a lot of fun, and I don't think we actually hurt anybody."

"Well, there is the matter of the insurance company," Rand said, "although the statute of limitation on that insurance fraud ran out long ago. And there's the shakedown of the university."

"No shakedown. It was on their own initiative that I got

the house and the stipend and all. Besides, they were paid back in the end."

"How's that?"

"By the life insurance policy they carried on me. As long as I died before I retired, while still paid faculty, they were the beneficiaries."

Rand put his face in his hands and shook his head. "Too many layers, deceptions within deceptions. I don't even know what to call that."

"Call it the way of the world. And call it time for cocktails. And then time for dinner. And then time for a moonlight walk on the beach. Give us a few days, and we'll make islanders of you yet."

☙

By the end of the three day visit, the two couples had become fast friends, and Shanna and Rand said their goodbyes with reluctance. In the taxi for the airport, Rand turned from watching the island stream by to look at Shanna. "Now we know their stories. What's next, for us, Shanna? Or should I say who's next? Who are you going to be? Is it back to being Toby?"

"Never. I'm going forward, not back, and not standing still either. And what's next for Shanna Newsom? Maybe becoming a wife and mother."

Rand drew back. "That's a real double, uh, double something. Wife? We haven't even talked about that. I haven't proposed. I mean, things are looking good, and all, but ..."

"Who says you have to drive? Who says I have to cook? I can ask you to marry me."

"And are you asking?"

"Nope, not yet."

"And the mother thing? You're not serious. I mean, aren't you too, uh …"

"Too old? You forget, I'm actually almost three years younger than it says on my driver's license."

"You don't have a driver's license."

"Oh, yes I do." She pulled a license from her purse and presented it to him with two hands as though it was a business card.

"When did you get a license?"

"Last week. It was easier than I thought."

He turned it over. "But this isn't valid. It's got the wrong address on Racine Circle."

"No, it's got the right address. I closed on the place at the top of the circle. The one for sale that has the yard and the big addition in back, three bedrooms. I've been feeling cramped in the bungalow."

"When did you do all that?"

"Last month. It was easier than I thought."

"Did you ever think to consult with me before doing this?"

"I thought about it."

"And?"

"I decided just to do it. Sometimes it's like that: a new driver's license, a new house, a new life. You know what I'm talking about?"

"And are we talking about having kids?"

"Not yet."

Appendix:

Always Me

Denton Reynolds,

a New England singer-songwriter known for his allegorical and elusive lyrics, made one of his last appearances at the Berkshire Buskers Music Fest in Massachusetts in 1996, where "Always Me" was his opening number. He is best known for "Teachable Moments," the title cut from his only album, a cassette release that included "Always Me" from a live recording at Passim in Cambridge, Massachusetts.

Always Me

Words and music by Denton Reynolds. Used with permission of Dented Rain Music, Ltd., and Seth Reynolds.

> A shade from the shadows
>   knocks upon the door—
>   demanding entry, demanding exit—
> reflection of a darkness from before.
>
> Chorus:
> That was me, this is me, this will be until I'm gone.
> The verses change, words rearrange, but the
>   chorus is sung on.

A voice from the echoes
  shouts across the space—
  demanding hearing, demanding witness—
sound within the noise of a distant place.

  (chorus)

A line from the chorus
  rings within the mind—
  demanding harmony, demanding counterpoint—
a melody beneath a dissonant rhyme.

  (chorus)

An image out of yesteryear
  hangs within the vault—
  demanding viewing, demanding insight—
portrait of the self includes the fault.

  (chorus)

A word from other stories
  speaks from off the page—
  demanding reading, demanding knowing—
truth beneath the lies from a separate stage.

  (chorus)

An act of ancient drama
  plays out within the now—
  demanding seeing, demanding healing—
reasons for the questions why and how.

  (chorus)

Acknowledgements

I owe both the genesis and the final form of this novel to my wife, Lucy. It was not long after the attacks of September 11, 2001, that she and I started talking about story ideas connected with the events, particularly about those people who were not in the spotlight but might have been in the shadows. It was the notion of becoming someone else, of assuming an identity, taking on and wearing the external being of another person, reinventing oneself, that most fascinated me as a writer.

Lucy moved on, going back to school in midlife to reinvent herself as a marine biologist and university teacher, which ultimately inspired me to return to this long-shelved story idea. For me, the mental breakthrough came when I realized the protagonist was a woman and her story was one of romance melded with mystery. I took on the task of helping to tell her story with some trepidation, but it was the right decision. I have never felt more fully immersed in a story or its characters.

I am truly, madly, deeply grateful to Lucy for her patience, indulgence, and encouragement, as well as for her insightful suggestions and sharp-toned criticisms that have helped make this book possible.

I also must once again thank my daughter Tovah for her patience and indulgence and sharp-toned criticism in the design of the cover. She helped me abandon a poorly conceived concept to move on to something that worked.

To that I would add my gratitude to USAF photographer Denise Gould, whose cover photograph is part of an impressive body of outstanding public-domain work she has created for the United States military. I wish I could thank her directly.

Finally, I want to thank fellow writer Mary Patterson Thornburg for taking time during the coronavirus crisis to give me insightful input that much enhanced the final version. Thank you, Miki, thank you.

About the Author

Lior Samson

is the pen name of a former university professor who has won awards for both fiction and non-fiction writing as well as for his innovative work in industrial design. He has more than two dozen published books, including thirteen novels and two collections of short fiction. As a consultant and teacher, he has traveled the world, lived in Australia and Portugal, and served on the faculties of two international universities.

He resides in Massachusetts with his family, where he cooks creative fusion cuisine and composes serious choral music. He is a freelance journalist and photographer and one-man technical support team for the three students in his life.

The readers who write with questions, kudos, and criticism are vital parts of the dialogue he seeks to spark through his writing. He enjoys hearing from readers and appreciates those who take the time to post reviews on Amazon and elsewhere. He can be reached by email at: lior@liorsamson.com

www.ingramcontent.com/pod-product-compliance
Lightning Source LLC
Chambersburg PA
CBHW022028240626
47154CB00007B/2313